PRAISE FOR THE INSPECTOR DAVID GRAHAM MYSTERY SERIES

"I'm in love with him and his colleagues."
"A terrific mystery."
"These books certainly have the potential to become a PBS series with the likeable character of Inspector Graham and his fellow officers."
"Delightful writing that keeps moving, never a dull moment."
"I know I have a winner of a book when I toss and turn at night worrying about how the characters are doing."
"Love it and love the author."
"Refreshingly unique and so well written."
"Solid proof that a book can rely on good storytelling and good writing without needing blood or sex."
"This series just gets better and better."
"DI Graham is wonderful and his old school way of doing things, charming."
"Great character development."
"Kept me entertained all day."
"Please write more!"

THE CASE OF THE BROKEN DOLL

ALSO BY ALISON GOLDEN

The Case of the Screaming Beauty (Prequel)

The Case of the Hidden Flame

The Case of the Fallen Hero

The Case of the Missing Letter

The Case of the Pretty Lady

THE CASE OF THE BROKEN DOLL

ALISON GOLDEN

GRACE DAGNALL

Cover Illustration: Richard Eijkenbroek

Published by Mesa Verde Publishing
P.O. Box 1002
San Carlos, CA 94070

Edited by
Marjorie Kramer

There is more treasure in books than in all the pirate's loot on treasure island.
Walt Disney

To get your free copy of *The Case of the Screaming Beauty*, the prequel to the Inspector David Graham series, plus two more books, updates about new releases, exclusive promotions, and other insider information, sign up for Alison's mailing list at:

https://www.alisongolden.com/graham

CHAPTER ONE

I T WAS A Saturday morning, and it was not starting out well.

Graham awoke feeling groggy, tired, and uncomfortable. In his dream, someone had been knocking repeatedly on the roof of his police car, either demanding help or just trying to annoy him, he couldn't tell which. He remembered trying to open the driver's door, but it was stuck or locked, and so he struggled fruitlessly with it while the knocking became louder and *louder*...

"Bloody pipes again," he grumbled, swinging his tired frame out of bed. The White House Inn suffered from an antiquated heating system that struggled to warm the old building, and its pipes knocked and clanged throughout each night. As he started his morning routine, Graham remembered that the same knocking sound had afflicted his dreams for the past few nights, ultimately waking and leaving him in a state that was decidedly unrefreshed. He looked in the mirror, frowning at the dark lines under his eyes. "I look a lot older than thirty-six," he told his reflection. It showed no signs of disagreement.

He showered and shaved as he always did, but he knew that nothing whatsoever would lift his mood until he'd had his morning infusion of high-quality tea. In truth, Graham had never planned to stay at the White House Inn for ten weeks, but the daily pleasure of coming downstairs to the dining room and sitting at his own table by the window with a big pot of Assam or Darjeeling still felt wonderfully indulgent. Every day one of the waiters – Graham knew them all by name now – would bring him a steaming pot of utter perfection, and the day would begin in earnest. His eyes regained a little of their sparkle just thinking about it.

This Saturday morning, it was Polly, a bubbly redhead. "What'll it be, Detective Inspector?" Try as he might, Graham could not persuade the staff to call him simply "Mr. Graham." Even an informal "David" would have been alright, given how long he'd been staying there. But after success with two high-profile murder cases and the recent celebratory article about the Gorey Constabulary in the local paper, his title had become a firm fixture.

"I feel like having something from China today, Polly."

"Isn't that how you feel *every* day?" Polly replied, grinning cheekily and standing patiently with her notepad and pen.

"That," Graham admitted, "is probably a fair comment. Lapsang Souchong, please. And make sure to bring the..."

"Timer. Yes, Detective Inspector." Polly scurried away to place the order and handle Graham's unusual request. There was absolutely no point, Graham insisted, in serving some of the world's best teas if the customer had *no idea* how long the tea had been steeping when it arrived at the table. His solution was to have the waiter start a small digital timer as soon as the boiling water came into contact with the tea leaves. That way, Graham knew when his tea was at its absolute peak. Some would have called him fussy. But on matters of such importance, he knew he was merely being *correct.*

Polly also brought the morning paper. The front page was splashed with reports of the celebrations marking Guy Fawkes Night, the annual commemoration of November 5th, 1605, the day that King James I survived an assassination attempt by a group of English Catholics.

This year, two evenings earlier, the town had fired off its biggest ever fireworks display. An impressive sum had been collected for local charities, and better yet the district hospital was glad to report only three minor injuries, far fewer than in previous years. Graham made a note to give his team a solid "well done" for their "Safe Fifth" safety campaign. He especially wanted to single out Constable Roach, whose idea it had been.

On the "Announcements" page, there were the usual births, marriages, and deaths – none suspicious – but it was just this relative peace and quiet that was beginning to bother Graham just a little. His first few weeks in Gorey had seen a pair of thoroughly unpleasant murders, requiring the very best from himself and the Gorey Constabulary, but in the last few weeks, their investigative powers had been focused on more routine matters like stolen cars, shoplifters, and the odd break-in. There had been a spectacular case of vandalism at the high school, but even there, little challenge was to be found. The guilty party had obligingly signed his name, for heaven's sake, at the bottom of the colorfully defaced wall.

Revitalized by the tea, Graham set off on the day's errand. He was determined to finish his Christmas shopping well in advance of the annual crush that he had been warned could make Gorey's small shops nearly intolerable.

As usual, he assigned a single objective to this outing: a suitable present for his now ex-wife.

"What's she into?" asked the first shop assistant he spoke to. "You know, hobbies? Interests?"

The question stumped Graham. He could hardly confess that he was looking for the kind of gift that might cheer up a woman who had barely smiled in months. "I think she'd enjoy something a little... *different*." When this was no help, he tried, "Perhaps something with some history? With a story behind it?" Graham was met with a blank expression.

The second shop was hardly any better and was even more crowded. "You mean," the female assistant tried, "like something used by a sleb?"

"A what?"

"A sleb. You know, a celebrity, a famous person."

Graham tried again. "Something that is special because of where it has been or what it was used for, as much as for what it *is*."

The assistant frowned. "Nah, I don't think we have anything like that." Then she bustled off to address a question about Christmas lights, and Graham searched fruitlessly before making his exit.

Further along, he came upon an antique shop, and after some thought, he decided to give it a try. "How about this?" the storekeeper asked, presenting him with a highly polished, eighteenth-century pistol. "Belonged to a notorious pirate, that did," he said proudly.

"Anything a little more... *peaceful*?"

In the end, he found what he felt to be the perfect gift. It was a small and beautifully detailed painting of Gorey Harbor, based, he was told, on a sketch found in the notebook of a priest who had lived on Jersey some four hundred years before. It showed the castle, splendid and dominating on its hilltop, above a harbor busy with fishing vessels, the old wharf, and a bustling fish market. "Eighty-five pounds," the storekeeper said. "But for a member of our brave Constabulary, let's just call it eighty."

As he was leaving with the painting neatly wrapped in brown paper under his arm, Graham noticed something that he'd overlooked on the way in. In the front corner of the shop's window was a doll dressed in an ornate, eighteenth-century nightgown, with curly blond hair and blue eyes. Something about it stood out. Perhaps he'd considered one of these dolls for his daughter's birthday one year?

No, that wasn't it. He pondered the doll as he made his way back to the White House Inn, past the three other shops he'd tried. And there in the window of one was a nearly identical doll, dressed the same way, but with black hair in neat braids. It was displayed just as prominently, right by the door.

Moments later, he saw another one. This one seemed older, slightly more worn, and hardly in saleable condition, and yet it stood prominently in the center of the window. He spotted two more staring out at him before reaching The White House Inn, and as he made his way through the front doors, he saw yet another. On the reception desk sat a pale-skinned, beautifully made doll in a green bonnet.

"Mrs. Taylor?" he asked, his curiosity welling up.

The proprietor looked up from her tablet, which she had been studying with an unusual frown. "Oh, hello Detective Inspector," she said brightly. "Been doing your Christmas shopping?"

"Indeed so, Mrs. Taylor, but I have to ask... These *dolls*," he said. "I'm seeing them everywhere. They must be in half of all of the shop windows. Am I imagining things?"

She clicked off the tablet and sighed slightly. "No, sir, you are not. But I'm surprised no one's told you about her yet."

"*Her?*"

"Beth Ridley," she said sadly. "Poor thing."

Graham was embarrassed to admit the girl's name meant nothing to him, but obviously it carried real emotional weight for Mrs. Taylor. "I'm afraid I don't..."

"She disappeared, you see. Ten years ago today. Only fifteen, she was. The brightest, nicest girl you could ever meet. She was well known around Gorey. Everyone loved her. Absolutely tragic."

"What happened to her?" Graham asked.

Mrs. Taylor shook her head. "That's just it. She was walking to school one morning and simply vanished into thin air. No phone call, no sightings, *nothing*."

"But surely there was a search for her?"

"Oh, goodness me, yes!" Mrs. Taylor replied. "They searched the whole island. All the woods and the beaches. The Coast Guard patrolled out at sea, looking for her. But all to no avail."

"So what do people think happened to her?"

Mrs. Taylor frowned darkly. "Well, not long after she disappeared, people started talking about her in the past tense, if you know what I mean, Inspector."

He nodded, his lips pursed. "Does her family still live on the island?"

"Oh, yes. Haven't you heard of Mrs. Leach?" The Inn's proprietor seemed to have extra time on her hands during this pre-Christmas lull. "The poor woman was beside herself, of course. Her only child, gone. Can you imagine?"

Graham didn't *have* to imagine, but he chose not to share that very private pain. He simply nodded again.

"So, the community rallied around her. Made sure she had everything she needed. Then some people at the Rotary Club, I think, set up a charitable foundation for her. People donated money so that she could keep the search going. She hired private detectives, forensic scientists, even sent experts over to Europe to look for her. None of it came cheap, of course, and I hear the private investigations have tapered off quite a lot lately, but her charity is quite well-known here, and a lot of people give what they can every month."

"Hmm, it's not uncommon for the parents of missing children to carry on the search and at least try to keep hope alive. Even when..."

Mrs. Taylor gave Graham a look that pulled him up short. "Hope springs eternal, Inspector. There are cases, you know, of kiddies going missing and then showing up in some basement years later..."

This, he had to concede. "It's rare, but it happens." But mostly, Graham thought morosely, there was a murderer who had thoroughly disposed of the evidence. Or had got lucky.

There were other possibilities, of course. A child could be spirited away to live elsewhere. Or they might have simply run, never making contact with those they were running away from. All over the country, the filing cabinets of "cold cases," those with no practicable leads, grew in number while grieving families could be told nothing to ease their pain.

"Poor lamb," Mrs. Taylor said in summary.

"But why *dolls*?" Graham asked.

"Oh, yes, I quite forgot. She collected them, you see. Had quite a number. Her uncle in America sent them to her. She had one in her bag when she disappeared, as I remember. The theory goes," Mrs. Taylor confided, "that the doll was somehow damaged in whatever struggle took place. Nothing but its leg was ever found."

"Its leg?" Graham said, thoughtful. He reached for his notebook but found he'd left it in his room.

She caught him as he turned to go. "Are you going to...? You know... Look into it?"

Graham smiled thinly. "I really can't say, Mrs. Taylor. It's a very old case, and we're short-staffed at the station."

"People hereabouts," she said, leaning in close, "would think the world of you for even trying. Not that they don't already," she added quickly. "But, you know, it would give her family hope."

"I'll see what I can do, Mrs. Taylor. Would you be an angel and keep our conversation to yourself, just for now though, please?" he asked politely.

"Of course, Inspector. You can rely on me."

Graham returned to his room and set up his laptop. Mrs. Taylor had not exaggerated the case's high profile or the extent of public sympathy. There was a Wikipedia page, a dedicated website, and all manner of opportunities to contribute to the Beth Ridley Foundation. Graham began bookmarking sites and taking notes.

As his research deepened, he became engrossed in it, and he quickly found himself greatly enlivened on what would otherwise have been just another Saturday afternoon.

CHAPTER TWO

O N MONDAY MORNING, Graham arrived a few minutes early, as usual, and found Constable Roach at his desk, taking a phone call. Roach took notes as he listened, and Graham decided to hover briefly and find out what the call was about. But as he did so, he noticed that there was – of all things – what he now knew to be an "American Girl" doll on the edge of the desk, by the stack of public information leaflets. Next to the doll, in a small, silver frame, was a photo of a girl.

"Missing person, sir," Roach explained as he replaced the receiver. "Our old friend, Mr. Hodgson."

Graham sighed. "Oh, God, not *again.*"

"Seems that he did a runner in the middle of the night, according to his long-suffering mother. She found his bed empty and called us straight away."

Graham set down his briefcase and slid off his jacket. Gorey's weather had become markedly cooler, and he was finding the extra layer indispensable in the morning hours. "Well, Constable Roach, why don't you utilize your growing investigative acumen and have a guess as to what's going to happen next?"

They both stared at the phone for a second, and then it rang. Roach listened for a few moments, extended his thanks, and ended the call. "What do you know, sir? Mr. Hodgson has returned! Alive and well, yet again."

"What's that, four or five times, now? Where do you think he goes?" Graham asked.

"Sleepwalking?" Roach offered.

"Possibly. But consider this: how old is our Mr. Hodgson?"

"Seventeen, sir."

"And what does that tell us about the likely nature of his nocturnal adventures?"

"Well, if he's anything like I was at that age..." Roach began.

"I don't need to learn too much about your personal life, Constable," Graham warned quickly.

Roach blushed. "I'd just say, well, *girls*, sir."

"Wouldn't surprise me for a moment. Pity someone can't clue his mother in to the nature of seventeen-year-old boys and their nighttime habits. Save us all a bit of bother. And, speaking of missing persons, I've been noticing these dolls all around town." Graham picked up the doll and then the silver-framed photo. "Beth Ridley?"

Roach's face fell. "That's right, sir."

Two and two added up quickly. "You *knew* her?"

"We were classmates at Gorey Grammar, sir. Went to the same youth group, too, for a couple of years. We all called her 'Barbie.'" Roach saw that his boss missed the reference. "Because of her blond hair, sir," he explained.

Graham replaced the photo and sat the doll upright on

the reception desk. "I'm sorry, Roach. That must have been terrible."

"If I'm honest, it still affects me. Especially at this time of year. It was such a *shock*. But it's nothing compared to what her mother's been going through, all these years."

Graham regarded the younger man with sympathy. "Mrs. Taylor gave me the basics. Have there been any new leads recently, or..."

"Nothing," Roach said simply.

Graham wasn't, in all honesty, the greatest fan of cold cases. The act of re-opening old files always felt like a slight against the detectives originally charged with the case, as though by simply re-examining the evidence, Graham was accusing them of being unprofessional. But with such strong public interest, not to mention Roach's own emotional connection, it was a difficult case to resist.

"Constable, how would you feel about helping me take another glance at the case file?"

Roach gulped before answering. *"Beth's* case file?"

"She deserves a few hours of our time, wouldn't you say?" Graham said. "Do we have the file here?"

"No sir, it's lodged at the Jersey Police archive in St. Helier. I could ask Sergeant Harding to pick it up on her way in, if you like."

"Ah, yes," Graham remembered. "She'll only have come back from Manchester last night. Did you hear anything from her about the computer course?"

"Not yet, sir, but there was something on Facebook about how she was becoming a 'digital warrior,' whatever that means."

"Sounds impressive," Graham chuckled. "Anyway, she won't be long. Cup of tea in the meantime?"

Roach put the kettle on while Graham placed a call.

"Marcus?" he asked.

"Good morning, Detective Inspector!" came the cheery voice. Marcus Tomlinson had already finished his second cup of morning coffee and was in tip-top form. "What news from Gorey?"

"Marcus, I'm going to give you a name from the past, just to see if it shakes any old branches."

"Fire away, old boy."

"Beth Ridley."

Marcus was quiet for a moment. "Ah. Well."

"I'm listening, Marcus." Graham reached for his notepad. "I mean, I know it's a hell of a long time ago, but..."

"No, it's not that," Marcus began tentatively. "I remember the case, clear as day. But, you see, I'm a pathologist. There was never a body."

"Of course," Graham admitted. "Just looking for a bit of context, that's all."

Tomlinson cast his mind back. "Well, this was your illustrious predecessor, of course. He did a thorough job of interviewing everyone. People spent hours at the house with Mrs. Leach and her then-new husband, Beth's stepfather... What was his name, now? Charles? Chris, maybe?"

"What happened to her father?" Graham asked.

"Oh, Bob Ridley? Haven't you heard of him?" Tomlinson replied.

Graham searched his memory, something that never took long. "Bloody hell, not the same Bob Ridley who's doing thirty-to-life in Wormwood Scrubs?"

"The very same," Tomlinson told him, impressed as usual with Graham's unfailing memory.

In one of Britain's most famous bungled robberies of recent years, Bob Ridley had shot a security guard to death before making off with cash and jewelry worth millions. When he was arrested after three weeks on the run, he claimed that he had fired the gun only to scare the guard away. Then he admitted that he'd "panicked," a word that proved catastrophic to his defense and very persuasive to the jury.

"I'm going to guess," Graham said, "that their marriage did not long survive his incarceration?"

"Not by even a day," the pathologist confirmed.

"Got it. Go on, Marcus," Graham said, already filling a page with notes.

"Ann Leach was a nurse at the hospital in St. Helier. I knew her just slightly. I signed a card to congratulate her when she got married again. The second husband passed away a couple of years ago. Brain tumor or something similar. Nothing fishy about it. But as for Beth's disappearance, it was a strange thing. Frightening. One day, she was walking to school, and then suddenly, she was not."

Graham put down his pen. "People don't just vanish into thin air, Marcus. I know the world is a strange and mysterious place, but I'm still a big fan of cause-and-effect when it comes to explaining what people do and why."

"True, true. I know that some suspicion fell on an old, homeless chap who used to sleep in the bushes near the Ridley house."

"Okay," Graham said, noting this down.

"But nothing ever stuck. Couldn't say if she ran away, was taken, or what. Very frustrating for the police at the time."

It sounded to Graham, at first blush, as though it would be equally frustrating for him. "Thanks, Marcus. I'll let you know if anything comes up."

"Tell you what, old boy," Tomlinson told him, "if you

get some movement on this, even a little, it'll mean a great deal to the people around here."

"Yes," Graham agreed, "that's what I've been hearing."

"Dinner on me at the Bangkok Palace if you even develop a new lead. No expense spared," Marcus offered.

"I'll hold you to that," he promised. "Cheers for now."

Sergeant Harding knocked on Graham's door, case file in hand. "Morning, boss."

"Welcome back, Sergeant," Graham said warmly. "How was Manchester?"

She mimed a shiver. "Cold, but there were some very nice pubs."

Graham let her have her fun. "And did you *learn* anything?"

"Oh yeah," Harding assured him. "Tons. I'll be doing some review this week, and then I'll give you a rundown on all the new databases we're going to have access to."

"Splendid."

"In the meantime," she said, setting the Ridley case file on his table, "are we *really* going to be looking into this?"

Graham flipped open the file, disturbed to find it so slender. "How would you feel about that, Janice?"

She glanced back at the reception area and then spoke to Graham in a whisper. "Roach was very, very upset about Beth going missing. It damn near wrecked his teenage years, I heard. He's still cut up about it. And it's not just him. Frankly, the whole place would thank you if you took another look at it, even if it didn't come to anything."

Graham was put in mind of several cases back in London, where the entire community – even those who'd never even met the missing child or the family – came out to help, to comb through bushes and search woodlands or who brought meals or money. There was something of the "Blitz" spirit in those gestures, a determination to stick together and see it through. Even, as was so often true, when there was precious little hope of anything but a tragic outcome.

"I'm with you, Janice. Let's get everyone copies of this file and see what we can come up with."

Harding headed toward the copier in her own office. "Including Constable Roach?" she returned to ask.

"Yes, certainly," Graham replied. "He's going to play a very important role."

CHAPTER THREE

ONSTABLE BARNWELL GRUMBLED at being directed to man the reception desk while the others discussed the Ridley case in Graham's office. "I've got plenty to offer, you know," he told Roach.

"Sure." The younger man was memorizing Beth's case file, line by line. "Sure you do, mate."

"I'm destined for higher things than this," Barnwell insisted. "Answering the phone. I mean, seriously."

Roach didn't look up. "If no one answers the phone," he observed, "how do we know when a new crime has been committed? One that might demand just the type of skilled police work for which you'll one day be famous?"

Barnwell adjusted his tie. "Are you takin' the mick?"

Finally, Roach stood, clicked his pen closed, and headed to the meeting in Graham's office. "Only a little. Shout if you need help, alright?"

Roach found Graham deep in thought, filling up his notebook quickly. "Ah, Roach. You up to speed?"

"Yes, sir." Roach and Sergeant Harding took seats while Graham jotted down a final comment.

"Right," Graham said. "So, not exactly a mountain of information to go on, is there?"

Harding shook her head. "If nothing was seen, nothing was reported, and nothing was written down, we end up with..."

"Nothing?" Roach guessed.

"Nearly so," Graham said. "We've got reports of two interactions that Beth had on the morning in question, between eight o'clock and half past. It was a Monday." He thumbed through his notes. "First, we've obviously got her mother, who sent her off to school just after eight as normal."

Harding picked up the thread. "Then there's Godfrey Updike, a retired civil servant who was caravanning with his wife. He saw Beth walking down the road."

Roach finished off what they knew. "Finally, we have Susan Miller, a classmate of Beth's. And mine," he added. "They walked to school together every morning, and Susan waited for Beth as normal."

"But she never arrived," Harding added. "Susan waited for ten minutes but then went to school on her own, assuming that Beth was sick."

"I suppose," Graham tried, "that Beth might have decided to skip school. You know, left home and walked in the usual direction, but then decided to do something else for the day?"

Harding pointed out a sheet in the slender file folder. "The school secretary told your predecessor, sir, that Beth missed a grand total of four days' school in the four *years* before she went missing. So we know she was fantastically healthy, and there's just no evidence that she was ever truant."

Graham nodded, making yet another note. "Yes, I saw

that, but there's a first time for everything." He changed tack. "Wouldn't it have been busy at that time of day? Surely someone would have seen something."

"Her route to school took her through a quiet, residential area before hitting main roads. The doll's leg was discovered in a street that would have been empty at that time of the morning. And people in their houses reported that they saw and heard nothing," Harding answered.

"Okay, what about a boyfriend?"

Roach was silent.

"There's nothing in the file," Harding said.

Graham turned to Roach. "Constable? Is there anything you can add?"

"No. She wasn't seeing anyone," he answered, his voice tight.

"Alright," Graham said. "So, like you say, this really isn't much to go on. I'm not proposing that we make this our top priority for the next week or anything, but I'd like to understand just why there's so very little in this file."

"Where do you want to start, sir?"

"Interviews," Graham said. "Let's talk to everyone again and see what shakes loose."

"Who should be first?" Roach asked.

"The mother. Ann Leach."

Harding was there first. "Happy to accompany you, sir," she said.

"Actually, Sergeant, I'd like you to take your new database skills out for a spin."

"Oh, right," Roach remembered, brightening up. "How was that fancy computer course up in Manchester?"

"Actually, rather good," Harding said. She was a little surprised at Graham's decision not to take her with him to visit Beth's mother, but she was keen to demonstrate what she'd learned on her course. "What am I looking for, sir?"

"Would it be completely unhelpful if just for the moment," Graham asked, "I say *everything*?"

She shrugged and then gave him a smile. "I'll do my very best, sir."

"I'm sure you will."

Graham turned back to Roach, who had gathered himself once more. Graham could see this case would tax the young officer's emotions, but he was also in a unique position to be helpful, and Graham couldn't pass that up.

"Constable Roach, I want you to come with me to see Ann Leach. In fact, you can make the call and set it up. See if she's home, and tell her we're just doing a routine review."

"Right, sir."

"Careful, Roach. I don't want you getting her hopes up over nothing. I'm just not satisfied with a case file quite so slender, and I want to build it up, if we possibly can. With me?"

"Loud and clear, sir. I'll make the call now."

Roach returned to the reception area, where Barnwell was dealing with his boredom by reorganizing the community noticeboard. He dialed Ann Leach's number. In Graham's office, Harding wanted a quick, quiet word.

"You're certain that Roach is the right person for this, sir?"

Graham motioned for her to close the door. "I know, Sergeant. He's going to have to deal with some emotions, and that's going to be tough. But he *knew* Beth, and her classmates, *and* her teachers. He's lived on Jersey all his life. If you were me, wouldn't you want that kind of resource to hand?"

"I would, sir. I'd just tread lightly."

"Depend upon it, Sergeant," Graham told her.

"Very well, sir." Harding's fondness for their two constables was something that she'd share only with Graham, but it was genuine, and she didn't want to see either of them hurt unnecessarily.

"Besides, I want to season him a bit, give him more responsibility."

"Yes, sir," Harding said. "But..."

"You don't agree?" he asked mildly. Opinions from his colleagues were twice as valuable when they were open and honest.

"I think it's great to ask for more from him," she said. "I just wonder if this is the right case."

"Noted, Sergeant," Graham said. "If I see things getting away from him, I'll be sure to make a change."

Harding nodded and headed back to her office, across the hallway from Graham's. She turned on her computer and pulled out her notes from the Manchester course. Perhaps, there was some new clue to be found in the plethora of data that was just becoming available to provincial police forces like theirs.

The software started up, giving her access to the Police National Computer and its numerous related databases. She typed in, "RIDLEY, ELIZABETH" and began to read.

CHAPTER FOUR

GRAHAM RANG THE doorbell of Ann Leach's well-kept home in one of Jersey's more comfortable neighborhoods, a mile or so from the center of Gorey. He was very aware of the American Girl doll in the front window, alongside a banner that featured a photo of Beth, smiling as she cut into a birthday cake. There was also contact information for the Beth Ridley Foundation. The door opened and a short, dark-haired woman with thick glasses answered.

"Ah. You're the police who called?" she asked.

"We are, Mrs. Leach. I'm Detective Inspector David Graham, and this is..."

"Well, bless me!" Ann exclaimed. "Isn't that little Jimmy Roach?"

Roach grinned, suddenly red-faced. "I wondered if you'd recognize me, Mrs. Leach."

"Oh, for heaven's sake!" she said, waving them in. "You're even taller than I remember. Well," she chuckled, "I suppose nearly everyone's taller than me. Especially these days. I swear I've shrunk six inches in the last ten years."

She invited them into a spacious living room that was nothing less than a shrine to her missing daughter. From left to right, around the three walls not occupied by a bay window, were photos of Beth arranged in chronological order.

Graham took a moment to take in the display. It began with Beth's birth, a newborn wrapped in a pink blanket with her exhausted mother smiling down at her. It progressed to pictures of her early birthdays, her first bike, and to her first day at primary school where she stood neat and grinning in her blue and grey uniform.

"This isn't the house we were living in when Beth, um, went...disappeared. We moved. To get away from the memories."

"Must have been a wrench," Graham responded.

"It was, but it was for the best." Ann gestured around the room. "This is how I remember. This is how I keep her memory alive."

Photos from holidays in France, on a rollercoaster at a theme park, on horseback, standing in a field with mud up to her knees, on a trampoline, all told of a full and active life. There was a tender portrait of Beth smiling on a summer's day. Her blond hair shone in the sunlight, almost luminous, and her blue eyes sparkled. But then the sequence stopped abruptly.

"I keep one more space," Ann explained, motioning to a gap by the doorframe. "For the photo of her homecoming." She gestured to the tan couch and they all sat down.

"Mrs. Leach," Graham began. "First, I'd like to express once more the deepest sympathies of Gorey Constabulary. As a relative newcomer to Jersey, your daughter's memory is being kept alive by the community in a way that I find very moving."

Ann nodded in gratitude. She was very slight, and looked perhaps ten years older than she otherwise might. This wasn't surprising. Parents of missing or dead children often looked much older than their years. Stress, he knew only too well, can age a face shockingly.

"We made the decision, on this anniversary, to review Beth's case file. I have to say, with no disrespect to my predecessors, that I find the file rather thin for a case of its kind."

"I'm sure they did everything they could," Ann allowed. "But a mother always wants them to do more."

"Well," Graham said, "I'm hoping that by going over old ground once again, we might unearth a little more detail, and perhaps add a few pages to the file. I don't have any new leads, I'm afraid. I don't want to give you the wrong impression."

"Thing is, you see," Ann began, "it won't make any difference to me whether you find a scrap of new evidence or not. I *know*," she said, fist in her palm, "that my Beth is alive. I dream about her. I hear her voice in her room. I hear her footsteps on the stairs. She calls to me, but she's always gone by the time I turn around."

Graham gritted his teeth through a painful moment before he was able to speak again. "Mrs. Leach, I want you to know that I understand *exactly* what you mean." Roach looked at his boss in mute surprise. "And it's out of respect for just that certainty that we'd like to ask you again about the day she disappeared."

Ann checked the wall clock and with a guilty smile, said, "I know it's only lunchtime, but you won't mind if I have myself a little G&T, will you?"

"Not at all," Graham said.

"Join me?" she offered.

"No, thank you," Graham replied.

Inwardly, this simple interview was a tremendous battle for him. The greatest pain a human being could be asked to bear was the loss of a child, and the memories of his own were never far from the surface. Such pain made his whole system cry out for relief, and a bottle of good gin, the familiar sound of the tumble of ice cubes into a glass, and the fizz of the tonic, all called to him like the mythical siren on the riverbank. He swallowed hard, gripped his notepad and pen, took a deep breath and began asking questions.

"Tell us about that morning, Mrs. Leach. What time did Beth leave for school?"

Ann's eyes were sad and distant for a moment, and then she sighed and began to describe the day she'd lost her daughter. "I made her a packed lunch, as I had every school day for ten years," she said. "Her uniform looked clean, and she had washed her hair the night before. She was a bit tired, but a cup of tea and breakfast seemed to give her some energy. You know how teenagers can be in the mornings," she smiled brightly, her eyes filling with tears. "She wanted to drop her doll off at Mr. Greeley's on her way to school. The leg was a little wobbly and he would do doll repairs for her on the cheap."

"Did she say anything as she left?" Graham asked.

"Just, 'See you later, Mum,' as she always said. You know, I've wracked my brains about every moment, and about every day before that, and I cannot for the life of me think of any reason..." She stopped, and for a moment it was all too much. She pressed her hands to her face and breathed hard. Roach shuddered slightly.

"We can come back another time, Mrs. Leach..." Graham began.

"No," Ann said, gathering herself. "You'd get the same

sad display. I've thought it through a thousand times, and I can't tell you anything to explain why she's not here with me, right now."

Graham glanced across at Roach, who seemed to take strength from Ann's fortitude. "Go ahead, Jim," he said quietly.

"Mrs. Leach, did Beth have anyone in her life who might have wished her harm?"

She shook her head.

"Please think about it for a moment, Mrs. Leach. Perhaps a former friend or a classmate she had a fight with?" The head-shaking continued. "Someone who claimed Beth had wronged them? Cheated them?"

"Everyone loved her," Ann said, her voice a thin wail.

"How well do you think she got along with her teachers?" he tried.

Ann thought for a few moments, drying her eyes with a handkerchief. "Her homeroom teacher was Mrs. Blunt," she said. "She was always very positive about Beth during parent-teacher evenings. Said she was a 'model student.'"

"Anyone else you can remember from her school?" Graham asked. Then he turned to Roach. "Who else taught your classes, back then, Jim?"

"Mrs. Wells," Roach said. "She was our math teacher. There was Mr. Knight, who taught geography and something else, I can't remember."

"And Mr. Lyon," Ann said, as if remembering after a struggle. "Her science teacher."

"Oh, yes," Roach confirmed. "He was a bit heavy on the homework."

Ann was nodding. "Yes, Mr. Lyon. I remember. He gave a lot of homework, and Beth used to go to the library after school to get it done. You know, they only had a handful of computers in the library back then, so two or three of the students used to share one and research the questions. Beth preferred books. She said she didn't have to wait for a modem to dial up, and she could just look things up in the back of a book."

Ann smiled a little at the memory.

As she was speaking, Graham noticed that in one of the more recent photos of Beth, there was a tall, heavy-set man with thinning, dark hair. "Could I ask about your late husband, Mrs. Leach?" Graham asked sensitively. "That's him, there, in the photo, isn't it?"

Ann didn't turn around. "Yes, that's Chris. He passed away two years ago last summer. Brain tumor. The doctors didn't see it until it was too late. Only twelve weeks, from diagnosis to funeral."

"I'm truly sorry," Graham said. "You must miss both of them terribly."

"More than I can say," Ann said.

"Did Beth get along well with her stepfather?" Graham watched carefully as Ann seemed to think this through at some length.

"Yes," she said. "He loved her very much. I know that she respected him and that she wanted us to be happy. To be together."

Graham made a note and in his own, personal hieroglyphics, inscribed the word "equivocation." Then he asked, "Do you have a room for Beth, Mrs. Leach?"

"Oh, yes. I've kept everything the same."

"I wonder if it wouldn't be too much of an imposition for us to see it."

Ann led them upstairs, apologizing for the mess in the other rooms. Ann's own bed was unmade, Graham saw to his surprise, and the upstairs part of the house could have used a lick of paint and a good airing out.

But Beth's room was immaculate. It wasn't so much a bedroom as a carefully arranged memorial. Every last object from Beth's original bedroom had been arranged just as it was in the Ridley's previous house.

"She collected dolls," Ann said. She showed them into the room, but she didn't follow. "She had nearly a hundred, but the American Girl dolls were her favorites. She was trying to collect the complete set," she recalled. "Lord knows how many there are in total." The dolls were arranged on Beth's bed in a neat display, their clothing pristine and positions neatly composed. "Her clothes, her books, everything is just how it was then."

While Ann waited outside, apparently unwilling to enter, the two officers looked around the room. Graham took his time, committing objects to memory – each book, each ornament, and the positions of the objects on her shelves. However, it was Roach who drew his boss' attention to an apparently innocuous green exercise book that sat with a pile of others on Beth's dresser. Rather than being entitled, "Geography 2004," or "French Vocabulary 2005," as others were, this book was simply inscribed, "SECRET."

"Her journal," Roach said quietly. "It was mentioned in the case file."

Graham thought back. "Didn't they dismiss it as... what was it? Plans for a cartoon, or something?"

"They thought they were notes for a children's book that Beth hoped to write one day," Roach replied. Graham opened the book and saw at once what his predecessors had meant. Over half of the book was filled with jottings that depicted the antics of various animals.

"You know what they say about a book and its cover,

sir," Roach said. "I think we shouldn't judge this by how it appears. I'd like permission to have a closer look if Mrs. Leach doesn't mind."

"Go ahead and ask, Constable. If you've got a hunch about this, I say we should follow it."

Roach made the request as politely as he knew how, and Ann immediately responded that he could remove anything that might be helpful. "Just provided," she cautioned, "that you return it exactly as you found it. No damage or markings."

"I promise, Mrs. Leach," Roach said.

There seemed little more to add, and so Graham led Roach downstairs to make their exit. "We appreciate your time. Please, if you think of anything that might be helpful, let us know."

"I think," Ann said sadly, "of nothing else for most of each day."

She showed the two men out.

"Good work with that journal, Constable," Graham said as they made their way to the car. "I wouldn't have thought of that."

"Like you said, sir. It's just a hunch."

CHAPTER FIVE

J ANICE HAD RELUCTANTLY agreed to man the reception area while Barnwell responded to a call from the marina. She was continuing her investigation into the missing girl's case on her computer. Even a month earlier, it wouldn't have been possible, but with their police computers now networked, she could interrogate national – and even international – databases from any of the office machines or her own laptop through a secure connection.

"The marina? What's going on down there?" she had asked Barnwell.

"Theft reported, last night," Barnwell said, pulling on his uniform overcoat. "Shouldn't take long."

Barnwell was very glad of any excuse to escape. He found himself willing the phone to ring or for the door to swing open and present him with an exciting challenge. Anything to interrupt another dreary day. Graham and Roach had the car, so he laboriously cycled the mile and a half to the marina. He'd have given nearly anything, he mused as he locked up the bike, to hear the squeal of his pursuit car's tires as he chased down a fleeing bank robber. But for the moment, this rather less dramatic assignment would have to do.

He strolled over to a man who was washing his boat with a long-handled, soft-bristle boat brush.

"Morning, sir. Looking for Captain ...," he looked down at the note he'd made, "Drake," he finished.

"Aye, that's me." Drake was a weather-beaten sixty-seven year-old who had spent as much time at sea as any man alive. He was a professional fisherman who knew the seas surrounding the UK, from Iceland to the Baltic to the coast of Portugal, like he knew Gorey itself. Drake waved Barnwell aboard his boat, *Clementine*. "Mind your step, now."

Clementine was a dedicated fishing vessel. "Just back from the German Bight," Drake reported. "Bloody awful over there, even for November."

"Did you catch much?" Barnwell asked. For someone who had lived in Gorey for the last six years, Barnwell knew shockingly little about the town's primary industry.

"Damn near bugger all," Drake cursed. "But once the weather settles, we'll be out there again. And again, and again until we hit our quota."

Barnwell noticed how neat and orderly the boat was, until he saw one glaring exception. The glass window of the pilot house was smashed. "Tell me about this," he said. "When did you notice it?"

"I slept ashore last night," Drake said, "but when I came down at six this morning, I saw some filthy bugger had made off with my doobury!"

Barnwell took out his notebook but then paused. "Your what's-that-now?"

"My GPS!" Drake said. "That digital doobury that used

to sit up by the wheel." He pointed to a now empty spot on the boat's dashboard. "Good kit, it was. Had sonar and everything! Worth nearly one thousand pound."

"You're insured, I hope," Barnwell asked.

"Course I bloody well am," Drake replied. "You ask the others. This kind of thing happens all the time. I tell you, there's not a decent soul left in the world."

"So there's been more thefts? Like this, off the boats?"

"Aye, happens all the time."

"But why don't they get reported?"

"Dunno. They usually take smaller stuff. But they're getting cocky now. And I don't like being messed with."

The hair on Barnwell's scalp started to tingle. Was he finally getting something to sink his teeth into?

"Alright sir, let's take down your statement, and I'll look into it straightaway."

Barnwell completed his notes and wrote a detailed statement for Drake to sign. "Thank you for reporting this so quickly, sir. We'll be in touch if we need anything else."

Drake grumbled something about wasted fuel and wasted time, bid Barnwell a gruff farewell and went back to his scrubbing.

When Barnwell returned to the station, he found Janice deep in a search on the reception desk computer.

"Let me have a moment on there, Sergeant, as soon as you can," he requested, cheerfully.

"Please," he added quickly as Janice turned to give him an arch look. His first line of inquiry would be one unavailable to previous generations of investigators who were chasing down a potential fence. "I need to have a little look on eBay."

CHAPTER SIX

IT TOOK GRAHAM and Roach only a few moments to track down Andrew Lyon, Beth's former science teacher. They discovered that he'd stayed in Jersey after leaving the teaching profession.

"Decided to make a career change, according to his website," Roach said, reading from his phone as Graham drove them to the address. "Sounds as though he's doing his own thing these days. Freelancing."

Graham kept slightly under the speed limit as they ascended the hill to the edge of the town and then turned left into a secluded street lined with some of the oldest trees on the island. "Nice spot to live," Graham observed to himself. It would not be long before he'd be searching for a place of his own. He couldn't stay at the White House Inn forever.

"What kind of freelancing?"

Roach skimmed a couple of online articles that carried Lyon's byline. "'Life in the Age of the Snooper's Charter,'" Roach read. "Looks like a detailed piece for an online cybersecurity magazine about how to keep the government's nose out of your Internet business."

Graham raised an eyebrow. "Interesting." He pulled up outside Lyon's house and turned off the engine.

"And here's another," Roach read. "Oh, you're going to love this one, sir," he promised. "'Putting the 'Dark' in Dark-Net: How to Browse Anonymously.'"

The DI took down a note as usual and then stepped out of the car. "Sounds as though our Mr. Lyon is someone who takes his privacy very seriously indeed."

"*Very* seriously, sir. You might say, to a professional level," Roach agreed.

"Well," Graham noted as they rang the doorbell, "let's see what he has to say."

The living room curtains twitched, and the door opened, "Yes?"

"Gorey Police, Mr. Lyon. Just a routine inquiry," Graham replied.

"Inquiry? What kind of inquiry?"

"It would be better to speak to you inside, sir," Graham told him, giving Roach a meaningful glance. "It's regarding the disappearance of Beth Ridley."

The reply was quick and rapid. "I don't know anything about that," the man said.

Andrew Lyon was in his late thirties, bespectacled but well-groomed, well dressed, and trim. Graham had been expecting someone pale and paunchy, a never-married white man with an indoor lifestyle and hobbies.

"I'm sure you don't, sir," Graham said, moving to his Plan B. "It's just that I'm new to the area, and with the anniversary of her disappearance this week, I'm trying to gain a little context from that period. Beth Ridley was your student. I just need a few moments of your time."

The man stared at them, then seemed to reconsider.

"Sorry," he said. "Please, come in."

As Lyon led them down the hallway, Graham glanced around, mentally cataloging what he saw. As he passed the living room, he noted white walls, polished hardwood floors, and two cream sofas facing one another. Chrome light fixtures were mounted on either side of the fireplace. Between them was a huge Dali print depicting melting clocks. The room was pristine. Graham revised his view of the man in front of him once more.

Lyon's office was dominated by his computer setup. It was also spotlessly tidy. Under the desk was a range of power strips, neatly labeled, their cables tied with green twine. In Graham's experience, computer cabling inevitably and without bidding took on a formation that made a plate of spaghetti look orderly.

"So," Lyon said easily, taking a seat in the office chair that faced his desk. He turned to contemplate the officers who were now seated on a couch, "how can I help you?"

He's like a Bond villain in his electronic lair, Graham thought as he began to speak. "Mr. Lyon, I'm sure you were as upset as anyone at the disappearance of Beth Ridley."

"I still am," he admitted. "She was smart. Engaged in her school work. Such a shock. There was nothing to suggest... It's something I've never really come to terms with. I donate to her foundation every month."

Graham turned to Roach who began to speak.

"Sir, I don't know if you remember, but I was a classmate of Beth's, in your Year-10 Science class." When Lyon did little more than stare at him, the Constable added, "Jim Roach, sir."

"Ah, yes," Lyon said uncertainly. "How are you, Roach?"

"Well, as you can see, it's Constable Roach these days. I wonder if you could tell us what you remember about the day Beth disappeared."

Lyon puffed out his cheeks. "It's a long time ago. I mean, for me, it was a day like any other, right up until I got the call that evening."

"Call?" Roach asked.

"That Beth was missing, and that they were asking for volunteers to come forward and help with a search," Lyon explained.

"And did you volunteer?" Roach asked him.

"Oh, yes. Like everyone else. We walked all over the island, it seemed to me. That night, the next day, the weekend, and for several weeks after. I used to hike a lot before my knee went iffy on me," Lyon explained. "So I knew the countryside around Gorey as well as anyone."

Graham interjected, "What was the mood like, among those who were searching for Beth?"

Lyon sighed at length. "It was bleak. You know, Beth's mother is absolutely convinced to this day that she is alive. But when you're on a search like that, looking under piles of leaves, in burrows, and in ditches by the side of the road, you're not expecting to come across Beth looking all rosy and healthy. We were expecting to find a body. You know what I mean?"

"Yes, I think so," Roach said.

"But there was absolutely no sign of her. I mean, we found some old clothing in a couple of places, but there was no reason to suspect it was Beth's. I think that they even did DNA analysis or something, but she was wearing her school uniform when she went missing, and we never found anything like that."

Graham pressed on. "How well did you know her?"

The question was very deliberate. It was calculated to provoke a response that might be very subtle indeed. Like a camera programmed to take shots in bursts of six or twelve, Graham watched Lyon's reaction in slow motion. He took in every nuance of Lyon's facial expression, every movement of his hands. How his eyes darted one way, then another, then skyward. How he licked his lips, which suddenly seemed dry. Perhaps only high-level negotiators, successful poker players, and police detectives shared this special skill; that remarkable ability to read a person's reactions in the minutest detail.

"She was a student of mine for two years," Lyon said. "But they were big classes, twenty-five or thirty kids in each."

Roach waited and then said, "So, you wouldn't say you were particularly close?"

Lyon suddenly glared at him. "Close?" he repeated. "What do you mean, *close*?" Lyon glanced at Graham, then back to Roach, his expression stern and offended. "What are you trying to imply?"

Roach softened his tone. "Nothing at all, sir. Just trying to establish how well she knew her teachers. How she got along at school."

"And just because she was my student, you think..."

Graham jumped in. "No, he doesn't think anything of the sort, and neither do I. Please don't worry, Mr. Lyon. We have no reason to suspect anything improper of you."

"I should think not," Lyon replied tersely. "With all these new laws and students reporting every last thing, the situation has become ridiculous," he said. "Just completely *ridiculous*. It was one of the reasons I got out of teaching."

Graham made a note: *Complaints against Lyon?*

"I remember," Roach said, "that you assigned a lot of homework."

Lyon blinked at the abrupt shift of topic. "I mean, yes. We couldn't possibly cover everything in class time, and the school used to make a great deal about exam results each year. If they didn't improve, we got the Spanish Inquisition."

"And do you remember Beth as someone who did her homework on time?"

Lyon shook his head. "I couldn't say. Like I said, she was smart, and I know she wanted to go to college on the mainland somewhere, but that's really all I remember."

Graham's attention moved around the room. He took in the DVD titles on the shelves, and then began surveying the photos sitting on the desk. Lyon featured in almost all of the photos. There was one of him kneeling at the center of a group of exhausted hikers, shrouded in mist at the peak of some unknown hilltop. He'd done a parachute jump at some point; there was the obligatory photo of him falling to earth, grinning at the camera with two thumbs up. And there was a pub photo, a table full of adults, smiling and raising glasses to the camera. Graham noted something and decided to ask about it.

"Do you still smoke, Mr. Lyon?" The house didn't smell of it.

"Quit," Lyon told him. "Four years ago. One of the hardest things I ever did."

"Did you smoke a lot, back in the day?" Roach followed up.

"Oh yes," Lyon admitted. "Pack-and-a-half a day for about ten years. Bloody filthy, I know, but it was just the best way to take a break in between classes. Helped when I was grading papers, too. Finally, I decided to clean up my act, and I feel all the better for it," he smiled.

They learned that Lyon had left the teaching profession after fifteen years and had begun freelancing as a journalist, writing for blogs and contributing chapters to those such-and-such for dummies books on computers, security, viruses, and the like.

"It pays the mortgage, just about," Lyon told them. "And I'm my own boss."

They found out nothing more, and eventually Graham thanked Lyon and drew the interview to a close. He led Roach to the outer hall. This time, Graham noticed a painting on the wall of the dining room. It was a classic Pre-Raphaelite scene of two young women by a riverbank. Both were naked, with alabaster skin and blond curls.

"Thank you for your time, Mr. Lyon," Roach was saying, "If you think of anything else, please be sure to get in touch." Lyon promised that he would and saw the two officers out.

On the drive back to the station, Graham and Roach silently considered the interview.

"What did you think, Roach?"

"I think he sounded a little too practiced, sir, but there was nothing concrete."

"Hmm."

"Do you think he's a person of interest?" Roach asked.

"Don't know yet, son," Graham said, "but we're going to find out."

Later that afternoon, with Barnwell and Graham gone for the

day, Janice was still at the front desk. Twenty feet away, Roach was working on his own search, one for which a computer was of little help. Given the use of Janice's desk, he was hunched over Beth Ridley's journal, reading and re-reading the neat handwriting. He had photocopied it, transcribed it, and made endless notes on what the strangely elusive text might mean.

"Okay," he muttered to himself, as was his habit when engrossed in a task. "We've got six characters, all of them animals." He counted them again. "Bug, Mouse, Puppy, Canary, Cuckoo, and Cat." His pen tapped rhythmically on a legal pad. "An insect, three mammals and two birds. What does *that* tell me?"

It had been his most frequent question since first opening the journal. How could this seemingly innocent, rather childish collection of half-stories possibly connect to Beth's disappearance?

"There's no hero," he observed quietly to himself, "but there's at least one bad guy: *Cat*." He circled the idea in his notes. "Cat is devious and scheming, always trying to take something that doesn't belong to him. Definitely a villain."

The journal repeatedly referenced Cat as "smelly" or "stinky." Puppy, on the other hand, was well-meaning and loyal but rather naïve. "*I wish Puppy would grow up*," Roach read from one of the last pages in the journal. And there, on the very last page, dated the day before Beth vanished: "*Puppy doesn't see the danger. She won't tell anyone, but I think I have to.*"

"*What* danger?" Roach asked himself.

Then, there was Canary, a flighty, unreliable character, and Cuckoo, who was selfish, taking things from others and calling them his own.

"Beth is never actually angry with Canary or Cuckoo," Roach concluded. "But she doesn't respect them at all."

Mouse, on the other hand, was even more naïve and lost than Puppy. "*Mouse gets eaten, but only because she chooses not to run away. Mouse is getting herself into trouble again. Cat loves it best when Mouse runs away, but only for a while. Then he chases, pounces, and Mouse is caught.*"

"Beth, dear girl," Roach whispered to the book, "what on *earth* are you talking about?"

The one element that did make sense was Beth's references to a character she called "Bug." "*Bug is kind and thoughtful,*" she wrote. "*Bug cares about me.*" And then, toward the end of the journal, "*Bug & Beth?*" The question was enclosed in a heart shape, shaded in with pink pencil.

It was the very strangest feeling to see his own nickname and his teenage self described in these pages. He sighed deeply, doing his best to stand back from the deep personal connection he had with the case. He and Beth had been closer than he'd felt able to admit to DI Graham, although their friendship had never had the chance to become anything more. Reading Beth's private thoughts made him feel deeply melancholy.

"Getting anywhere, Jim?" Harding asked from the doorway.

Roach snapped back to the present with a sudden jolt.

"Sorry. Didn't mean to scare you," Harding added, taking a seat opposite him.

"You need your desk back?" Roach asked, rubbing his eyes.

"It's six-thirty, Jim. I'm headed home. I'm surprised you're not on your way to practice by now."

"Oh!" Roach said, suddenly, noticing the clock. "Oh, shoot! Is it Monday?"

"It's been Monday all day."

Roach rose from the desk quickly and stumbled around,

finding his soccer bag under the reception desk and apologizing before dashing out of the door. He was trying to secure a regular starting place in the Jersey Police five-a-side squad. They were defending the championship title, and the coach would make him do extra push-ups if he were late.

Once he was gone, Janice closed out her own workday by logging off and checking around the office. "Are you cracking the *Da Vinci Code* or something here, Detective Roach?" she observed dryly to herself as she perused the desk Roach had been working at. She tidied up Jim's notes and placed them in a manila folder. "Good for you, lad."

She turned out the station's lights and locked up. Barnwell would be on call tonight in case of emergencies. Janice tossed her bag into the back seat of her MG and started the car. She felt not a little lonely as she considered the evening ahead of her. "A girl like me," she reflected as she backed out of the station's small parking lot, "should be on her way to a hot date."

The car roared reassuringly as she found first gear and gave it some gas.

"Yeah, right. Dream on, Janice."

CHAPTER SEVEN

THE ONLY CALLS Barnwell usually received in the middle of the night were dire emergencies, burglaries, or crank calls from bored people who couldn't sleep. At daybreak, though, he was often informed of crimes that had happened overnight and were only now becoming apparent. The call from Captain Smith was just such a report.

"Good morning," Barnwell said, locking up his bike.

"I wish it were a better one," Smith replied, stepping off his boat and approaching Barnwell. "And I wish I still had my searchlight, too."

The boat owner showed Barnwell bright, new scratch marks on the light's mounting, which was empty now but still bolted to the outside of the pilot house.

Barnwell started making notes. "You know, I was only down here yesterday. You're certain it was here last night?"

Smith stared at him as though Barnwell had suggested the experienced fisherman might have forgotten how many limbs he had or possibly the names of his children. "Certain as Christmas," Smith replied. "Some bugger came along with a screwdriver and half-inched the damned thing. None too neatly, neither."

Des Smith was another weather-beaten old salt, even more leathery than the older Captain Drake. The two had been in a good-natured, decades-long competition, plying the unpredictable seas in a bid to consistently bring home a larger catch than the other. Smith's crew was a mix of younger men, including several sons of retired captains, and a couple of old-timers who had a few years left in them. As Barnwell approached him, he could see that Smith was dressed in a woolen sweater, fisherman's overalls, and was smoking a battered pipe, the very image of the Ancient Mariner.

"There's been a rash of these thefts," Barnwell told him. "Captain Drake's GPS yesterday, and now..."

"I *know* that, lad!" Smith exclaimed. "What I want to know is this, how can it happen here, night after night? This is why we need some kind of protection, dammit."

Security at the marina was a topic of contention. Gorey Police were woefully understaffed for such a task, while the consortium who owned the marina had imposed cutbacks after three straight years of financial losses. The first thing to go had been private security. They hardly saw the point in spending money to protect a dozen boats whose best days were long behind them. In response, the boat owners had withheld their dues and threatened legal action, leading to an unhelpful standoff.

Barnwell closed his notebook after taking Smith's statement. "We'll do what we can," Barnwell promised. "I can't be certain that these thefts are related, but it wouldn't surprise me."

This didn't impress the veteran fisherman. "We need to bring back public pillory," Smith announced. "Stick 'em in

THE CASE OF THE BROKEN DOLL   47

the stocks in the middle of the market square and throw bad eggs at 'em. See what happens to the crime rate then!"

"I'll take that under advisement, Captain. In the meantime, you and the other boat owners might think about organizing a watch at night, just in case."

Just as Drake had done, Smith grumbled something profane and returned to his boat.

Barnwell jumped back on his bike and headed to the station, but as he cycled away, he was struck by a thought.

"Oh, hell." He turned the bike around and peddled straight back to the harbor.

"You caught him already, then?" Smith hollered as Barnwell approached.

"On second thought," Barnwell explained, "I'll stand watch tonight." The reception desk phone would be forwarded to him if he pressed the right buttons. "I'd like the thief arrested, not chopped into fish bait."

"Right y'are," Smith replied and smiled, revealing teeth Barnwell considered he wouldn't want in his own mouth. "Good luck with catching the bugger."

Back at the station, Sergeant Janice Harding was patrolling cyberspace on the hunt for Andrew Lyon. His employment history came up easily enough, largely due to the standard Criminal Records Bureau checks that were a requirement for teachers. She read through his credit history and found the dates of two property purchases. He lived in one home while leasing the other to a young family on the island. No complaints or incidents were on record for either, so she moved on.

The IP address relating to his home was listed on

several Internet business databases, and it was straightfor-
ward enough to track down which websites he worked on.
And that was when she began taking very detailed notes.
Twenty minutes later, she called Graham.

"I'm on my way to the school, Sergeant," the DI
explained. "What's new there?"

"Well, sir, I've been investigating Mr. Lyon, like you
asked."

"Yes, good," Graham said, the noise of the car's engine
rumbling in the background. "Anything interesting?"

Janice cleared her throat. "*Interesting* is one way of
describing it, sir."

"Oh?"

"Well, put it this way. Once I'm finished with this, I'm
going to take a long, hot shower."

"Ah," Graham said. "I did wonder if our Mr. Lyon
might have a tendency toward the... how shall we say..."

"Prurient?" Janice tried.

"Well, you tell me," Graham replied.

"Not on the phone," Janice decided. "I'll give you as
graphic a rundown as you can handle once you're back at
the station."

"Understood, Sergeant."

Roach was doing the driving, and his curiosity was
piqued. "So, Mr. Lyon's a pervert?"

Graham winced. "Picture a cart," he said patiently,
"and now a horse. There is only one proper order for those
two things, wouldn't you agree, Constable?"

"I would, sir. It's just that... well... I thought there was
something not quite right about him."

Graham sighed. "It takes a lot more than a thought,
Constable."

"Yes, but..."

"And, these days especially, it's a *hell* of an accusation to throw around. You know how many teachers have found their careers ruined because one of their students even *suggested* some kind of impropriety?"

"Too many," Roach agreed. "But how many students have been suffering in silence because they thought no one would believe them?"

"Difficult," Graham admitted.

They were reaching Gorey Grammar, the school Beth and Roach had attended. It was housed in a neat Edwardian building surrounded by well-kept playing fields. A game of field hockey was underway, and they could hear the coach's encouragement booming across the open space.

"Schools should be the safest environments we can make them," Graham was telling Roach as they got out of the car and crunched across the gravel toward the school's impressive entrance. "But it's misleading to call someone a 'pervert,' just as much as it is to call them a 'criminal.' You can't boil a complex human being down to a single word. Still less should that single word define your view of them or how they're treated by the law."

"Interesting point, sir," Roach conceded.

Jim had climbed the steps before him hundreds of times as a teen, and being at the school once again was making him feel nostalgic.

"Anyway, you're an alumnus, so you can do the talking," Graham offered.

"Thank you, sir. But I don't know how much they'll be able to tell us, this far removed."

They were greeted in the lobby by the head teacher, Liam Grant. He was almost impossibly tall, a thin beanpole of a man, pleasant but reserved, with a broad Irish accent. He didn't appear overly thrilled to have police officers on the premises, especially when one of them was in uniform, but he was friendly enough.

After Roach had made the introductions, Graham asked Grant, "Were you head of the school when Beth was here?"

"Oh no, I was a wet-behind-the-ears English teacher back then. Straight out of teacher training. I had no contact with Beth."

Graham nodded.

"But I've asked Mrs. Wallace to talk to you. She's our school librarian and been here for nearly twenty years. The library is this way," Grant said, keen to escort the two investigators through the echoing hallways before the end of class.

"The place will be thick with students in a few moments, but they don't tend to spend their break at the library, so it will be quiet in there."

Roach was hit by a wave of memories as the three men walked down the corridors. They still had polished, wooden floors and rows of battered lockers opposite each classroom. He thought back to his old school friends, teasing each other, laughing about last night's TV, worrying together about exams.

They passed the classroom in which Jim had spent a whole year. He struggled to remember any more than five or six faces from that young crowd of twenty-five who had been as close to him as family back then. *Simon, Susan, Paula... What was the name of the little spindly kid? Ah, yes. Brian "Shady" Sycamore. Wonder whatever happened to him?*

Somewhere in those memories was Beth, but at that moment, all he could picture was the brightness of her blond hair with the sun behind her through the window.

Very little about the school seemed to have changed, until he saw the library.

"This used to be like the reading room of a monastery," Roach observed aloud. "And now it's more like the deck of the Starship Enterprise." Rows of computers occupied most of the library's old, wooden tables. But it still had that quiet, restrained air. The shelves of books stretching back into the depths of the spacious room felt very familiar. As they entered, two boys who had been poring over a large book at one of the tables seemed to take this as their cue to leave. They closed the book and left it on the table as they headed out.

"Funny you should say that, Constable," Mr. Grant noted as the two young men filed quietly past him. "This used to be the school's chapel, until the need for a library became sufficiently great. Now, the books are being usurped by computers and handheld devices, but it still retains that calm, other-worldly atmosphere, don't you think?

"Anyhow as I said, I'm really not sure how helpful we can be, but Mrs. Wallace was here when Beth went missing. As the librarian, she gets to know just about all the students. You're welcome to look around as much as you need to."

Grant left them in the company of the librarian whom Roach remembered from his time at the school.

"Things have changed, Mrs. Wallace," Roach said.

"Indeed they have." Mrs. Wallace turned to explain for Graham's benefit.

"Back in 2005, we only had two computers, and only one of those was connected to the Internet. The number of times I had to dash over to remind the groups to *share* the mouse..."

Roach chuckled at a memory. "Good times."

"Beth usually sat here," she said, indicating a table by

the window. The view from there was over the largest of the playing fields and the woods beyond. "She didn't care for the computers. Worked from her class textbooks or others she took from the shelves."

"Did she come to the library alone, Mrs. Wallace?" Graham asked.

"It varied. Sometimes alone, sometimes with her friend, Susan Miller. They would sit side by side. Susan would usually leave before Beth, but Beth always stayed on until we closed."

"What time was that?"

"Five o'clock. Beth was always the last to leave."

"Did she talk to anyone while she was here?"

"No, I remember her as being very focused on her work."

"Were you involved in the search for her, Mrs. Wallace?" Graham asked.

"Oh, yes," she replied. "Terrible thing. Only time in my life I can remember when success would have meant disaster."

Roach was nodding. "Do you recall anything from that time that might help?"

Mrs. Wallace paused and cleaned the glasses that hung from a chain around her neck.

"You know," she said, "we all speculated about her. Probably a terrible thing to do, but with no witnesses or evidence, we were bound to start guessing. I remember thinking to myself that she might have been keeping a secret. Something she couldn't tell anyone."

"What kind of secret might that have been?"

But Mrs. Wallace wouldn't be drawn out. "Speculation," she repeated. "Just trying to make sense of the incomprehensible."

"Please, Mrs. Wallace," Graham said. "We don't mind a little guesswork from time to time."

The old librarian leaned in close. "I think there was a *boy*, you see. Someone who wasn't at this school. And I've had it in my head ever since..." she said. "Oh, I know it's the silliest thing, but I just have the *feeling* that she'd got herself into trouble. You know, couldn't tell a soul. I think that they went away together, her and the boy, had the baby, and now are living out their lives, unable to return." She told her version of events in a rapid, hushed whisper.

Roach, who had stiffened at the librarian's hypothesis, thanked her. After confirming that this was all Mrs. Wallace could offer them, he escorted Graham out to the playing fields. "Interesting idea, but I wouldn't put it at the top of our list," Roach said.

"Agreed, Constable."

"It's a cliché, sir, I know, but..."

"She 'wasn't that type of girl?'" Graham guessed. Through the recollections of others, the family photos at the Ridley's house, and Beth's own belongings, he was building a picture of a girl who was seldom caught on the wrong side of the rules.

"Not even a little bit," Roach confirmed. "She really didn't have a reputation for being too friendly with the boys. In fact, we were all a little in awe of her."

"Smart, capable females are terrifying to teenage boys," Graham said. "Grown up boys, for that matter," he added. "I think you're right that Mrs. Wallace is being a little too creative. Been reading too many of those romance novels, I reckon."

They walked back into the school building. Classes had restarted, and they were surrounded by the all-too-familiar sounds of education: teachers calling names, chairs scraping hard floors, the clattering of students pulling books from their school bags.

"Amazing how little things change," Roach said.

They went outside and as they reached their unmarked police car, Graham brought out his notepad for a final update.

"So, what's next, sir?"

Graham spent a moment in thought, and then something seemed to click in his mind. "Hang on a minute. We've been idiots."

"Have we?" Roach asked, surprised.

"Come with me, lad. I can't believe this, but we've ignored the most priceless source of information at any school."

"What?"

"Not *what. Who.*"

CHAPTER EIGHT

GRAHAM KNOCKED ON Mr. Grant's office door and soon discovered that his thought was correct. "Of course," Grant confirmed. "Couldn't run the place without Mrs. Gates. Her office is right next door, actually. This way."

Roach gave his boss a puzzled look. "Old Mrs. Gates is going to be our star witness?" he whispered.

"What makes you doubt that?" Graham asked as Grant knocked on the school secretary's door.

"Well, she was about two hundred years old when I was here, back in the day. I don't know if she'll even..."

"Constable, have you ever known a school that *didn't* have a long-serving school secretary who knew everything about the place?"

Mrs. Gates was closing in on retirement, an event that would clearly precipitate a giant upheaval for the school. Aged sixty-three, and possessed of an institutional knowledge that stretched back to the nineteen seventies, Mrs. Gates had an encyclopedic knowledge of staff and students. "Well, goodness, of course I remember Beth," she said.

"Bright, full of energy and talent. The Lord only knows what happened to her."

"Well," Graham said as they took seats in her small but highly organized office, "that's why we're here. I'd like to find out as much as we can about Beth's time at the school."

Mrs. Gates nodded for a moment and then pushed back from the desk to unlock a filing cabinet in the corner. "Every year," she said, flicking through a drawer crammed with manila folders, "they inform me that these records are going to be put on the computer. And every year, we find another excellent reason to leave a perfectly good system well alone. Aha," she said, pulling out a slender folder.

"Another thin file," Graham muttered to Roach. "Just once, I'd like something the size of a phonebook."

"Elizabeth Victoria Ridley," Mrs. Gates announced. She handed over the folder.

"Good grades," Graham noted. "A after A, with the occasional A-minus."

"Damn near perfect attendance," Roach added. Then he lowered his voice. "Doesn't sound like the kind of girl who'd get herself 'in trouble,' does she?"

Graham was nodding, memorizing the file. "She had Mr. Lyon for two years in a row," Graham noted.

"Nothing unusual about that. The science courses are a full year long," Mrs. Gates told him.

"True," Roach recalled. "And a long year, it was too. And I still couldn't tell you why the moon has phases or why the sea is salty."

"That's because you were too obsessed with sport to pay proper attention," Mrs. Gates reminded him.

Roach blinked. "That was ten years ago!" he marveled. "How could you possibly..."

But Mrs. Gates simply tapped her temple and smiled.

"Told you, didn't I?" Graham muttered. "Mrs. Gates," he said, turning back to her, "I wonder if the school still has records of which teacher was on duty in the library after school? I'm assuming that was the practice?"

"Oh, yes," Mrs. Gates confirmed, making a beeline for another filing cabinet behind her desk. "Especially after we got the new computers. And there was that incident with the Year 11 boys."

"Incident?" Roach asked. Then, the memory suddenly came to him. "Oh *yes*, I know what you mean..."

"Terrible," was all Mrs. Gates would say.

Roach had a smirk on his face. "I only ever heard the rumors, sir, but it seems that a group of senior boys decided to have a poetry session at the very back of the library after school one day."

Graham raised an eyebrow. "A poetry session, Constable? Sounds a little unlikely."

"Well, this was *Jamaican* poetry, sir. With, erm, appropriate herbal accompaniment."

Graham stifled a laugh.

"Stank to high heaven!" Mrs. Gates complained. "Mrs. Wallace said it was like walking into a Rastafarian commune. Took us *days* to get the smell out."

She finally located another folder and handed it to Graham. "Here. Teachers still volunteer for library duty. It means that they're exempt from morning assembly or some other odious task. Back then, though, there was overtime allocated to it. If they needed a bit of extra money, teachers could sit in the library, overseeing the students while doing some grading or class prep."

Graham scanned the document quickly, unsurprised to see one name reappearing throughout 2004 and 2005. "Mr. Lyon seems to have done more than his fair share of library duty," Graham noted. "He was there at least once a week, sometimes twice."

"He was always angling for more money. His dream was to be his own boss. I don't want to tell tales, but I know he wasn't the greatest fan of our head at the time."

"Who was that?" Graham asked.

"Mr. Bellevue."

"Is he still around?"

"Only in the cemetery. He died of a heart attack the Christmas after Beth disappeared. I always liked him myself, but he and Mr. Lyon had professional differences. Mr. Bellevue expected a very special level of dedication from his teachers. Andrew was forever getting himself distracted by some plan to get rich. He liked to buy property and lease it."

Graham wrote all this down. "The original folders say there was no record of Beth being at school that day. Can you confirm that?"

"I can. She wasn't present for any of her classes." Mrs. Wallace, seemingly from memory, pulled out the attendance registers for each of the classes Beth had had that day. There was an "X" next to her name in each one.

"Well, thank you, Mrs. Gates. I think we have all we need for now, you've been very helpful," Graham brought the interview to a close.

Roach followed his boss back to the car. "So," he summarized as they got in and the car rolled slowly along the school's driveway, "there's no evidence that she made it to school on that morning. Everything points to the fact that she disappeared off the street on her way here."

"Yup, that is the logical conclusion," Graham agreed.

"But Lyon pulled a lot of extra library duty. To save up for a second house, do you think?"

"Or for some other reason, perhaps," Graham agreed.

"He did give a *heck* of a lot of homework," Roach pointed out.

"Knowing full well," Graham said, "that Beth and others would spend time in the library."

"Right where he would be." The thought was an uncomfortable one. "Is it a bit less presumptuous of me now," Roach asked, "to call Mr. Lyon just a little *creepy?*"

Graham drove them back at a slow, steady pace, deep in thought. Finally, he said, "I'm reluctant, Constable, really I am. He could have given a lot of homework precisely so he'd get the overtime to buy his second home or whatever his current scheme was. Or there could be no ulterior motive at all. We are speculating again. Where's the evidence?"

Roach looked at him, skepticism written all over his face.

"It's possible," Graham finally conceded. "But let's see what Sergeant Harding has got for us."

CHAPTER NINE

JANICE WAS DRINKING a cup of tea when they got back. "Barnwell's at the marina again," she explained, "so I'm holding the fort."

She pulled a face.

"How's it going?" Graham asked, taking off his long coat and hanging it up behind his office door.

"Well, sir, put it this way. If things were different, and I worked for a company where the bosses check their employees' browser history, I'd be in big trouble right now."

Graham pinched the bridge of his nose.

"Okay," he said, "Roach, would you cover the desk? Sergeant Harding, let's use your laptop. I don't want these things in my browser history."

He waved her into his office. "Roach, check in with Barnwell and see that he hasn't fallen into the harbor or something."

Harding pulled up a chair and turned the screen so that it faced away from the door. "Okay. I hope you're ready for this."

Graham brought out his notebook. "Roach is certain

there's something not quite on the up-and-up with Lyon," he reported.

"Well, sir, I tend to agree with him. I've turned up a whole lot of information about Mr. Lyon that would support his conclusion. The annoying thing about it, though," Harding told him, pulling up her research on the laptop, "is that it's all circumstantial. He's *definitely* creepy, no doubt whatsoever about that. But I can't prove that the filthy man has actually broken any *laws*."

"How do you mean?"

"Exhibit A," Janice said. She brought up a website. "The street address for this is in Denmark. Lyon has worked for these people for about three years. He designed their payment system, the front-end, and their shipping and tracking software."

"What do they do?" Graham asked, but as he clicked through the site, it became abundantly clear. "Oh, for heaven's sake."

"High-end, luxury bondage gear," Janice said, somehow managing to keep a straight face. "Whips, chains, you name it."

"I'd prefer not to dignify it with a name," Graham said. "Not my cup of tea, Janice, but I don't think it's against the law. What else have you got?"

"Well, there's this thoughtful group of contemporary artists," Janice said, clicking a bookmark that brought up a website dedicated to an "adult videographers' collective." I haven't downloaded anything, but the thumbnails might clue you in."

Graham peered a little closer and then wished he hadn't. "Legal?" he asked.

"Oh, yes," Janice replied. "All the required language is there at the bottom of every screen. Everyone's eighteen or over, pursuant to this section of that law, so on and so forth. As far as I can tell, the site is kosher, both in Denmark and in the UK. Which is a shame," she added, "because Lyon built almost all of it."

There were three other sites on similar themes, but nothing about them suggested that laws were being broken. "Immoral, arguably, but sadly not illegal," Janice concluded. "Mr. Lyon remains decidedly creepy, but we don't have a case against him."

"Not yet," Graham said ominously.

Janice frowned. "Sir, I've done a pretty thorough search here. Everything on the database is—"

"There's more," Graham interrupted. "I'm sure of it. But it won't be easy to get. When we do, I have a feeling it will be a great deal *more* than circumstantial."

He reached for the phone. "And I know just how we can get it."

Barnwell sighed heavily. He had come to detest riding around on the bike, however good for the environment or his own health it might be. There was something laughable about it, something weak and childish. He always felt over-weight and uncoordinated on the damned thing, even after losing ten pounds in the last couple of months. He felt sure that one of these days, he'd crash into someone or tip himself into the harbor like an idiot.

As it was, the traditional modes of police transport – the horse, the patrol car and, most dynamic of all, the motor-cycle – carried a note of authority. His bicycle simply announced the fact that Jersey police were underfunded and couldn't afford a second car for the Gorey force.

He locked up the bike, mopped his brow, and headed into a shop. Immediately adjacent to the harbor were a group of businesses that catered to professional fishermen and day anglers, as well as pleasure boat owners and scuba types.

"Afternoon," Barnwell said. "Is Mr. Foley in?"

For the last twenty-five years, Arthur Foley had made a living supplying Gorey's boating community with the myriad essentials of maritime life. There were huge tubs of bait, coils of rope, endless shelves of books, and big racks full of maps and charts. Furthermore, he sold every electronic gadget a mariner might ever need. Barnwell had been called out to investigate yet another theft. Immediately on spotting the glass case full of GPS devices and other expensive boat technology, Barnwell suspected that he knew what had been stolen.

But he was quite wrong.

"The blighters were away before I could even shout at 'em to stop," Foley explained. "They just strode in here, bold as brass, grabbed two cans of paint, and legged it."

"Paint?" Barnwell said.

"Aye. Not the kind of thing you'd decorate your kitchen with, either. Specialist paint for boats."

"Boats need special paint?" Barnwell asked, reminded yet again just how little he knew about the sea and those who plied their trade upon it.

"Gawd, yes," Foley explained. "Dutch company. Makes a range of paint that repels barnacles. Bloody magic, actually."

"What?" Barnwell quipped, "The barnacle takes one look and decides he wouldn't be seen dead on a boat with such a garish color scheme?"

Foley rolled his eyes but patiently explained. "It's chemistry. The barnacle can't stick to the paint."

"I thought every boat in the world had its fair share of limpets and such," Barnwell said. "Went with the territory."

"Aye, but it's bloody expensive," Foley told him. "You ask any of the old boys outside how much extra fuel they'd need because the streamlining of their hull was all shot, owing to barnacles. Slows them down by as much as a knot."

"Interesting." Barnwell said, "You know, I've learned a lot since I started investigating these thefts. Tell me about the shoplifters."

"Came in, looked around, found the paint, grabbed the cans, and buggered off like greased lightning," Foley repeated. "They were wearing those 'hoodie' things, so I couldn't see their faces."

"Do you have CCTV?" Barnwell asked, but Foley's facial expression gave him the answer.

"Costly," was all he said.

"Very well. I'll do my best, Mr. Foley. But it would help if you could take a stab at how old they were."

"It'd only be a guess," Foley told him. "Early twenties? I mean, they ran off at quite a pace."

"Height?"

"About five foot eight, nine, I'd say. The other was taller, nearer six foot."

"Build?"

"Both slim."

"Anything else you can tell me?"

"Nope, can't say that I can."

"Well Mr. Foley, if you see or hear of them again, be sure to give us a call. I'll ask around and see what I can find out about these two, but I suspect they're the same ones who are nicking stuff off the boats at night."

"Yeah well, I hope you catch 'em soon."

Barnwell finished his notes and took his leave of the shop owner before clambering back on his bike and making his way to the station.

On his arrival, he found himself warmly welcomed by Janice.

"You're back! I thought you'd run away to sea," she exclaimed.

"Hilarious. I was called out to the marina again. They've had another theft down there. Paint, this time. That's two in one day. They're getting bold." Barnwell explained.

"Eh?"

"See, I've been thinking."

"Always dangerous," Janice interjected with a wry smile.

Barnwell ignored her. "I figure," he explained, "that there are three types of thief. The first type nicks things because he wants to sell them. Either to order or speculatively. Part of a plan or spontaneously."

Janice grinned as she typed another search into her laptop. "'Speculatively' and 'spontaneously,' eh? I think those are the longest words I've ever heard you use, Constable." Barnwell continued to ignore her, concerned only with expounding his theory.

"The second are those thieves who need the thing for themselves. In this category, I might include those who steal specialist boat-hull paint. It doesn't really make any sense otherwise."

"And the third?" Janice asked, reaching for her tea.

"Kleptomaniacs. Those who get a kick out of stealing.

Wouldn't even matter what the goods were. It's all about the thrill."

Janice closed the laptop. It was about time to head home, and she'd done all the digging on Lyon and Beth Ridley's disappearance that she could for one day. "Couldn't kleptomania explain your paint thieves' behavior? They saw that security was poor and that they'd probably get away with it. Chose something portable to pinch."

"Sure," Barnwell allowed. "But there were a couple of them. Be unlikely to find two such weirdos in a small place like this. And why *paint*, of all things? I mean, there are plenty of other items in that store. Books, maps, fishing tackle boxes, boots, oars, you name it. But they chose something heavy and practically useless to anyone who isn't refurbishing a boat."

Janice packed her laptop into her satchel. "I think you're answering your own questions, Constable." She regarded him sympathetically. "Are you going to be at the marina tonight?"

"I told them I would," Barnwell sighed.

"Better you than me."

Barnwell nodded ruefully.

"Well, night, Bazza," Janice said. "Don't do anything I wouldn't do."

Barnwell took off his uniform cap and ran both hands through his short, brown hair. He glanced around the marina, where he'd spent the last three silent, freezing hours achieving absolutely nothing, and made sure he was alone.

"Bugger," he said with sincerity.

It had been a tedious night, one he was anxious not to

repeat. There had been no signs of break-ins or likely thieves, only a drunken tourist who would probably have fallen into the harbor if Barnwell hadn't shocked him into sobriety with a flashlight and a judicious telling-off. The man staggered back to his hotel, full of apology and whiskey, once more leaving Barnwell to contemplate the deserted boats tied up at the wharf.

He'd already considered and roundly dismissed the notion that the fishermen were in cahoots with one another, pulling some kind of insurance scam. It just didn't fit with what he knew about them. They were fundamentally decent souls, wedded to their boats and the sea, far more willing than most to put themselves in danger in order to put bread on the table. He knew that the local fish stocks were depleted, but that didn't mean these old salts would descend to insurance fraud to make ends meet. He just couldn't see it.

No, this was targeted thievery by someone who knew what they were doing and what they wanted.

Aching and exhausted, Barnwell unlocked his bike and reluctantly hauled himself into the saddle.

As he was contemplating this disappointment, he spotted movement out of the corner of his eye. He turned to see two figures, both in dark clothes and wearing hoods. They were beating a hasty retreat from one of the boats at the far end of the wharf. Each of them held an oar.

"Oi!" Barnwell bellowed. "Stop right there!"

The two thieves bolted at an impressive speed. Barnwell cursed the confounded bicycle, turning it laboriously around and then peddling as quickly as he could along the pedestrian area that ran parallel to the boat slips. He gained speed quickly, his blood now singing in his veins.

"Gorey Police!" he shouted. But the two were swift,

dodging between parked cars as they headed into the alleyways behind the shops that lined the street. They disappeared so quickly, he figured that they'd probably worked out an escape plan in advance.

Barnwell reached the shops and cycled around for a few minutes, hoping to catch the thieves breaking cover. There was no sign of them until he spotted two shapes in an alley opposite the Flask & Flagon, one of his favorite pubs.

He brought the bike to a squealing halt and leapt off as quickly as his bulky frame allowed, leaning the bike against the wall and proceeding down the alley.

"Gorey Police!" he shouted again. "Show yourselves!" He shone his flashlight down the alley and then winced at the sight.

"Oh, for heaven's sake," Barnwell growled. There was a sheepish smile from the woman and a terrified expression from the man.

"Get yourself home to the wife quick before I call this in." The man mumbled a quick thanks as he sidled past Barnwell and out of the alley. "And you should know better," he said to the woman. "Get going, and don't let me see you around here again unless you want to do another thirty days."

"I'm going, I'm going," she confirmed, before quickly leaving.

Barnwell returned to the bike and leaned against the wall. He was more exhausted than he should have been after a half-mile sprint on the bike and was furious that he had let the thieves get away. He checked left and right and saw that he was alone.

This time, he said it with real feeling. "*Bugger.*"

CHAPTER TEN

I T TOOK NEARLY an hour after their arrival for Roach's stomach to settle down. A crossing from Jersey to the port of Weymouth, on England's south coast, made for a pleasant jaunt in summer, but in November, it could be hellish. The ferry had been tossed around, the sea sufficiently rough to have a good number of passengers reaching for sick bags. Roach was among them, embarrassed to be quite so stricken in front of his boss. One elderly passenger, seemingly immune to the rolling, pitching, heaving experience, commented dryly that a uniform and a badge did little to protect someone from the forces of nature.

"Reminds us that we're all equal before the Lord," the old man said. "Something to think about."

"I'm mostly thinking," Roach confessed as he breathed deep and hung onto a rail for dear life, "about trying to keep my breakfast where it should be."

Graham fared better, although deliberately overdosing on seasickness medication had left him groggy. They stopped at a café so that he could take on a pot of tea, after which he felt nearly human again.

"Did you get anywhere with Beth's journal?" Graham asked, just before requesting the check.

"I did," Roach said, showing more enthusiasm than he had thus far that morning. "I've identified at least two of the characters," he said. He chose his words carefully. He didn't want his closeness to Beth and appearance in her journal to jeopardize his place in the investigation.

"Good lad. Who are they?" Graham asked.

"'Canary' is her mother," he said with certainty. "She's attractive and bright, but not particularly deep or thoughtful."

Graham smirked a little at this. "I reckon a lot of teenagers would make similar criticisms of their parents."

"I certainly did," Roach admitted.

"Although canaries can signal a problem before anyone else realizes there is one. They can be pretty astute. Useful, too."

"And I'm pretty sure that 'Cuckoo' was her stepfather, Chris."

"Ah," Graham said. "The pretender who makes use of the nests of other birds. Very clever."

"As for the others, I think 'Puppy' might be a school friend who was especially immature, but I can't link the name to anyone. And 'Mouse' is another friend, someone who's making a lot of mistakes."

"Good work, Jim," Graham said, leaving cash in a saucer on the table. "Alright, Constable, let's have a quick word with Mr. and Mrs. Updike." They left the café, "And then I'm afraid it's back on the boat for us."

Roach took a look back at the port. It was enough to bring on a new wave of nausea. "Can't wait, sir. Really."

Godfrey Updike and his wife of fifty-one years, Petunia, lived in a row house about three miles from the port. Graham hailed a cab and re-read the pages from Beth Ridley's case file that described their original statements from ten years before.

"He saw Beth walking to school, and they had a short conversation," Graham summarized.

"Not much to go on," Roach said. The cab ride was bringing his nausea to the surface once more. He couldn't wait to sit on the Updikes' sofa or in fact, on anything that wasn't *moving*.

"I suppose we'll see. It's a bit of a long shot," Graham said. "You feeling alright?" he asked, concerned at the greenish tinge that was shading Roach's face.

"Will be, sir. Don't you worry."

Graham paid the taxi driver, and they found themselves standing in front of the Updikes' home. "Seeing as you're not feeling your best, I'm happy to do most of the talking," Graham offered.

"Righto."

As soon as Godfrey Updike opened the door, Graham realized that despite outward appearances, this was not an ordinary row house in Weymouth. "Good afternoon, there. Jersey Police I presume," Godfrey said, and then chuckled amiably. "Welcome to our little museum."

Shelves, alcoves, cabinets, and every other available surface were all crammed with ornaments and knick-knacks. Graham's encyclopedic mind went into immediate, involuntary overdrive, cataloging the vast array of objects. There was simply nowhere for the eye to rest.

"Come on through to the living room," Godfrey said after the introductions were handled. "Petunia's just working on something. Can I offer you some tea?"

"I'd never say no to that," Graham smiled.

Updike was now seventy-six, according to the file, but was sharp of mind, with clear blue eyes and a straight back. Godfrey gave the impression of a man given to rigor and order and Graham immediately suspected a military background, although that was at odds with the fussiness that surrounded him.

"Petunia, love, those two police officers from Jersey are here." His wife, a beaming woman with curly white hair, was sitting on the sofa, painstakingly assembling a three-inch tall scale model on a lap tray. "Can we tear you away from William and Catherine?" her husband asked.

"And little George!" Petunia pointed out. "Forgive me for not rising, gentlemen," she said. "But I'm waiting for William's glue to dry." Graham peered at the orderly assemblage of pieces and tools on the tray; the box for the mini-diorama showed Queen Elizabeth alongside the British monarch's grandson and his wife on the balcony of Buckingham Palace, exhibiting their new son George to the world.

"Coming along nicely!" Godfrey announced.

The Updikes' home was nothing short of an unofficial annex to a royal museum. Commemorative plates, mugs, tankards, paintings, models, books, photos, posters, and innumerable other objects showed that their enthusiasm for the British Royal Family had wandered toward the obsessive.

"We spoke briefly on the phone," Graham reminded the couple as Godfrey took a seat beside his wife.

"Yes," Godfrey remembered. "You're reopening the investigation into Beth Ridley."

Graham cautioned him politely. "I wouldn't go as far as that, sir. The anniversary of her disappearance is this week, and I was just a little disappointed to see such a paucity of information in the case file. We thought it was time for a review of the case."

Graham brought out his notepad. It was a reflex action, like a smoker reaching for his lighter. "For the moment, we're just trying to flesh out our understanding of what happened on that morning."

"Well," Godfrey recalled, looking down at the beige carpet, "Petunia and I took our caravan to Jersey every year for... What would it be, love? Ten years or so?"

Petunia explained, "We got a little bored of the Dordogne and fancied a change of scenery somewhere a little closer. Back then the South coast and Channel Islands were our stomping grounds. These days, we head over to the Brecon Beacons, sometimes the Cotswolds."

"We love the caravan, you see. Cost effective and we can do as we please," Godfrey added. "If we're not enjoying the scenery, we're following the Royals around," he added.

"Following them?" Graham asked. He glanced around the room, every wall reminding him of the Updikes' abiding fixation with the monarchy.

"You know, we follow their diaries and turn up to see them arrive at their official engagements. We like to wave to the Queen as she goes to church when she's staying at Balmoral in the summer or Sandringham at Christmas," Godfrey said with a smile. "That kind of thing. It's like a hobby."

"Once, she was gracious enough to wave back at us," Petunia added proudly.

Graham shifted in his seat, more than ready to move on from these anecdotes and return to the point of their visit.

"How long had you been on Jersey prior to the day that Beth went missing?"

"That was the Monday, wasn't it?" Godfrey said. "Our last day there. We were due to head back up on the afternoon ferry."

"And when did you see Beth?"

Godfrey's eyes narrowed as he recalled the details he could still remember. "I left the caravan at about ten past eight or so, after the news headlines had finished. I remember thinking that we needed a few things for the journey home, and that I'd pop into the newsagent. I was crossing the street when I saw her."

"What do you remember about her?" Graham asked, noting down Godfrey's recollections in a sequence of detailed hieroglyphs.

"Pretty," Godfrey said. He glanced at his wife but she said nothing. "Tall for her age, I'd say. She had a black rucksack over her shoulder, and just as I was crossing the road, she stopped and looked inside it."

"What happened then?" Graham prompted.

"She brought out a doll. It had brown hair and a green dress, I think," Godfrey narrowed his eyes as he remembered. "She seemed to check or confirm something, and then walked off with it in her hand."

"Did you speak to her?"

"I called out 'Good morning.' She turned and smiled at me. That was it."

"What time was that?" Graham asked.

"It was about a five minute walk to the newsagents so I'd say, what, 8:15? Naturally, once I came out again, she had gone."

"How long were you inside?" Roach asked.

"There was a line," Godfrey recalled. "People buying their papers and such like. Probably ten minutes, all told."

Graham was nodding. "And that was the only time you saw her?"

"Yes, we left an hour later to catch the ferry."

"Godfrey likes to be there in plenty of time," Petunia explained. "He gets very agitated when the clock is ticking and he's afraid of being late. There was a time when we went to see the Duchess of Kent and—"

Her husband tapped his wife on the arm. "They don't need to know all my little foibles, dear." Then he said to the two officers, "I wish we could be more helpful. It's just terrible, the whole business."

"Any eyewitness report is potentially useful," Graham pointed out.

Godfrey rose with surprising agility for a man of his age. "I don't suppose you'd like a quick tour, before you leave?" he asked. "Seems a shame to head straight back so quickly after such a long journey."

Frankly, a tour of the house was the last thing the two officers wanted, but they acquiesced, and Godfrey showed them around the remarkable, crowded little museum that he and his wife had built over their fifty years together. Perhaps their proudest possession was a dinner plate from the wedding of Prince Charles and Lady Diana in 1982, signed by the head chef.

Downstairs were numerous photos of the Queen Mother the couple had taken, including a close-up of her during one of her last public engagements. Upstairs, there was collection of figurines depicting the royal families of generations past, as far back as Queen Victoria.

Graham was frustrated. This interview had, thus far, only confirmed what they already knew. No new information had come to light. He was feeling antsy, and this guided tour around the Updike's home wasn't easing his mood.

He allowed his gaze to wander, taking in details but discarding most of them automatically. As collections of royal memorabilia went, it was superb, but it was hardly germane to the Beth Ridley case.

Then, quite when he least expected it, an object jumped out at him. It was in a box, on the bottom shelf of a battered, old corner unit. It was partially hidden by a host of other dolls and figures, apparently awaiting repair.

"Do you collect dolls, Mr. Updike?" Graham asked, leading the old man to the corner of the upstairs landing.

"Oh, those are some of Petunia's old projects. Been there for years. They're not part of our display. Now this," he said, lifting a ceremonial tankard from a shelf by their bedroom door, "was presented to us by the Prince of..."

"Would you mind terribly," Graham asked, "if I took a quick look at this box?"

Roach had already spotted the doll Graham was interested in and had his phone out, camera ready.

"Of course," Updike said. "Nothing very interesting, though."

Graham pulled out a doll, naked with brown hair. He noticed at once the manufacturer's mark on the back of the neck: *American Girl.* It was in less-than-perfect condition, but Graham could see it was the same type as the dolls he'd seen in the shop windows in Gorey, and among the huge collection on the bed in Beth's room.

Graham turned to Updike. "I'm afraid," he said slowly as Roach began to photograph, "that I can't agree." Graham turned the doll to ensure that Roach could photograph the most important detail of all.

One of its legs was missing.

CHAPTER ELEVEN

"MR. AND MRS. Updike, I'm going to ask a simple question, and I'd like a simple answer."

"Of course," Petunia said. She had made the tea while Godfrey gave the officers their tour, and Graham found himself distracted by the aroma. "We're happy to help in any way we..."

"Is there anything more you'd like to tell me about the morning you saw Beth?"

The elderly couple looked at each other. "It happened just as I said," Godfrey replied. "Petunia, love, did I forget something?"

She was shaking her head. "You told him just what you told the police back then," she said. "Almost to the word."

Graham looked at the Updikes, sitting there with their perplexed expressions, surrounded by the countless collectibles that made up their earthly possessions. They were rather an *odd* couple. Eccentric. He'd known elderly couples who lived extremely private lives, indulging in whatever hobbies suited them best. But none of those couples had ever seemed remotely capable of a serious crime, let alone abduction or murder.

"I don't think there's any other way of putting it than this," Graham said. "The doll upstairs matches the description we were given of a doll Beth had in her bag on the day she disappeared."

"But..." Godfrey spluttered, "what can you mean?"

"And now, it seems, an identical doll is in your house," Graham pointed out. "Minus a leg. Did you know a doll's leg was found on the street from where we believe Beth went missing?"

Roach observed the couple closely. If they were faking their utter astonishment, then they were accomplished actors. He'd never seen people quite so stunned in all his life.

"They made *thousands* of those dolls," Petunia objected. "*Hundreds* of thousands! They were the most popular brand in the world for a *decade!*"

"Longer," Godfrey added. "How many of them are now missing a leg, eh? Hundreds upon hundreds. Cast aside, damaged, stolen by the family dog, torn apart in a childish fight over property."

"Where did you acquire the doll?" Graham asked. Roach glanced over at his boss' notebook and saw two words, in block capitals and underlined, among the dense, incomprehensible scribble: *BROKEN DOLL*.

Petunia blinked over and over, her hand covering her mouth, deep in thought. "Was it a flea market?" she asked herself. "A charity shop?"

"But why," Graham said, too impatient to wait for her answer, "did you purchase a doll with a missing leg?"

Godfrey smiled slightly. "Petunia enjoys her projects," he said. "You know, fixing things up, finding replacement parts. Her specialty, for many years, was finding *just* the right replacement for a teddy bear's missing eye. Besides there's a market for these refurbished dolls. They're not cheap!"

Petunia was still deep in thought. "A collectors' fair, maybe? The one in Abbotsbury?"

Graham kept his frustrations to himself, but having made such an apparently vital discovery, the old couple's vacillating was a huge annoyance. After ten long years without progress, the case was finally bearing some fruit, and yet Mrs. Updike could only sit there, dithering and second-guessing herself as though she'd lost all her marbles at once. "Constable Roach and I are pressed for time," he explained. "We need some answers."

But nothing would come, however hard Petunia appeared to be trying. "I'm sorry," she muttered. "It was so many years ago, and I..."

"*How* many years ago?" Graham said, his frustration beginning to well up dangerously.

Roach glanced up at his boss with a flicker of worry. "I'm sorry, Mrs. Updike," he said, far more gently than his boss, "but it's important." He tried to catch Graham's eye, in a bid to calm the DI's mood, but Graham was fixed resolutely on the flustered elderly woman while he waited, his temper steadily rising.

"I... I really couldn't say," Petunia stammered. Then she looked at Graham pleadingly. "You can't possibly think that we had anything to do with... you know... that poor girl. Godfrey just saw her in the street that morning. That's all there is to it." Her face showed something close to panic at the thought of having become a suspect.

"Mr. and Mrs. Updike, we will need to remove the doll for forensic examination. Taking your age into consideration," Graham said, "we won't be requesting that you accompany us to the station. But we advise you to stay in Weymouth. Please don't travel outside the area so that we can contact you, should we need to."

"What?" Godfrey said, aghast. "This is all just so unnecessary..."

"As the investigating officers," Graham said sternly, "*we* will decide what's necessary. You should know that this is the first concrete lead we've had in the last ten years."

"Lead? A lead?" Petunia was even more disturbed than her husband at this unexpected turn of events. "Godfrey, what must they think of us?" She looked at her husband imploringly and began to weep. Her husband put his arms around her.

Graham took a deep breath and softened his demeanor a little as they got ready to leave. "Look, the forensics tests will take a few days. I'm sure you understand, in a case of this nature, that we have to take any evidence very seriously."

Petunia was by now in a flood of tears that she was unable to stop. "It's just a doll!" she wailed. "A one-legged broken doll that no one wanted."

Ignoring her pleas, Graham left his contact details and reminded Godfrey not to arrange any travel until the tests were concluded. "We'll be in touch," Graham said as they were leaving.

Roach heard this as an ominous warning as no doubt did the elderly couple who were left badly shaken.

Graham said little on the cab ride back to the port, where they arrived just in time for the late afternoon ferry. "Don't forget your seasickness pills this time, Constable," Graham advised.

"Already took three," Roach told him.

"How many are you supposed to take?"

Roach glanced at the package. "Erm. One." Roach paused for a moment. "Sir?"

"Yes, Roach," Graham was staring out to sea, deep in thought.

"Were they telling the truth, sir?"

"Perhaps. We'll know more when we have forensics look at the doll." He glanced at Roach.

"It's just that, sir..."

"You think I was a little harsh on them?"

"Yes, sir."

"Hmm," Graham looked out to sea again. "Maybe I was, Constable."

Twenty minutes after boarding, Graham closed his notebook after much ferocious note taking. He turned to Roach to ask his opinion on the Updikes and their doll. It was an objective that went unmet.

The sea was much calmer on this return journey, but Roach had learned his lesson. There was no likelihood of an opinion from him on the Updikes or on anything. Graham's young colleague was completely, deeply asleep.

CHAPTER TWELVE

D I GRAHAM AND Sergeant Harding were sitting together in his office when the call came through.

Graham listened for a moment and then asked a few questions. He made notes, checked his email for the file he was expecting, and then clicked through to it quickly. "Right, sir. Thank you."

Harding read the screen alongside him. "Wow," was the first thing she said. "I knew they could do this kind of thing, but I never thought we'd be able to..." She continued reading. "Oh, *wow*."

The document was a list of every website visited by Andrew Lyon in the previous eighteen months, and to a criminal investigator, it made very interesting reading. "The first thing to note," Harding said, making instant use of her new skills, "is that he's a frequent user. You see all these sites highlighted in red?"

"Yeah," Graham noted.

"Those are the ones the Home Office and the

Metropolitan Police have decided are basically... well... illegal websites, sir."

Some were just strings of letters and numbers, but others had names that left Graham in no doubt as to the kind of content one might find there. "Then there are the blue ones," she said. "They're not actually *illegal* as such, but they're close enough that they're banned in some countries."

Graham scanned the list. "He's on one of these, sometimes a whole string of them, pretty much every night."

"They're web forums, sir," Harding told him. "I can show you one that is relatively innocuous if you like."

"Is it going to appear in *my* browser history, Sergeant?" he asked.

"I'll show you on the laptop, sir." She opened her own machine and typed in the address. "See?"

It was one of the sites Lyon frequented the most.

"Has he broken the law?" Graham asked. He wanted to "see" as little as possible.

"It all depends on what evidence we're able to gather," Harding explained. "We've got records of him downloading files from the illegal sites," she said, opening a spreadsheet with hundreds of entries. The filenames alone were emphatically incriminating. "This data though, without other evidence, probably won't be enough for a jury. That said, at least he can't blame anyone else."

"How do you mean?" Graham asked.

"Lyon lives by himself, so he can't claim that someone else uses his Internet connection."

Graham frowned. "It's undoubtedly progress," he said, "but it's hardly 'game, set and match,' is it? All this tells us, really, is that he has some unusual proclivities." He glanced back at the screen and then averted his eyes. "Can we close all this down for a moment?" he asked. "It's not helping me think this through."

Harding did as requested but sent the list of websites to the printer. "If nothing else, sir, we'll be able to scare the hell out of him. If this got out, it wouldn't do his reputation much good with the local community."

Graham looked at Janice sternly for a moment but said nothing. He brought out his notepad. "So, we've got a powerful method of putting pressure on Lyon."

"I'd say," Harding agreed.

"But you know as well as I do that we can't arrest someone simply for downloading a file."

Harding frowned. "I think that it's ridiculous, but yes."

"*Possession* counts, Sergeant. Anything else is just circumstantial evidence. A jury isn't going to convict him based on his browsing history. He would have to *own* copies of the images, and in this day and age, that means they have to be on his hard drive."

Harding didn't like this one bit. "But we *know* for a fact that he downloaded them. He wouldn't download the files and then not open them would he?"

"Probably not, but we have to *prove* it."

Janice sighed.

"He downloaded the files, but that's not enough for him to see the images," Graham continued. "I've worked on cases like this before, and the loopholes are enormous. We'd have to prove that he unpacked the files and stored them on his hard drive or on a removable disc. That's the only evidence a jury would find compelling enough to convict on."

"That's crazy," Harding concluded.

Graham rubbed his eyes. "I don't disagree, Sergeant, but we're constrained by the laws as they currently stand. Juries tend to see records like *these*," he gestured at the screen, "as second-hand evidence, a *report* of an event, rather than direct evidence of the event itself."

Janice puffed out her cheeks. "I mean," she sighed, "do they *want* us to catch these creeps, or not?"

"The person I want to catch," he reminded her, "is the person who caused Beth Ridley to go missing. I don't know if Lyon's adventures on the Internet relate to that in any way, but it does point to an unfortunate interest in young women and girls, and that's the line I think we should take with him. Let's lose this battle," he gestured at the screen again, "in order to win the war, eh?"

"Might it be a good idea to have another chat with him? Ask for an explanation? Even just to shake him up a bit?"

A small kitchen timer trilled on Graham's desk, and he stood to walk the few paces to the corner cabinet where a teapot stood ready. He poured a cup and savored the aroma before turning to Harding. "With all that you've shown me, we could probably get a warrant to seize and search his hard drive," Graham said. "But he's not our only suspect."

Harding thought for a second. "Don't tell me that you've got something on that old couple in Weymouth?" Harding asked.

"They had a doll, as near as I could tell *identical* to the one Beth was taking for repair on the day she vanished. It was also missing a leg."

"Wow," Harding breathed.

The station's front door opened and Roach appeared. "Morning," he called.

"Morning, Constable," Graham turned to Janice. "Roach has been tracking down a homeless man who was sleeping in the bushes near Beth's home around the time she disappeared. We need to chase that lead down, too, *before* we take any action on Lyon. And we still haven't spoken to the friend who walked to school with Beth every day. This has a long way to go, yet."

Roach came to Graham's office door. "So, I've found him," he announced with a certain pride. "His name's Joe Melton, and he lives on Guernsey. With your permission sir, I'd like to head over there this afternoon and see what he has to say for himself."

"Granted," the DI said, "as long as the water's calm. Don't want you out for the count again."

"Got anything more on Lyon?" Roach asked.

"Not half," Janice answered.

"Don't tell me, let me guess. He's a complete pervert."

This time, Graham made no move to disagree. "Creepy," he confirmed. "Uncommon interests."

"Hmph," was all Roach said.

"But," Graham said, a finger aloft to caution against speculation, "he's not the only suspect, and we still have other leads to chase down. Right, Constable?"

"Yes, sir," he said. "Guess I'm off to Guernsey, then."

"You are indeed," Graham replied, "and while you're doing that, Sergeant Harding and I will speak with Susan Miller."

CHAPTER THIRTEEN

THEY CLIMBED THE stairs together, making their way to the third and highest floor. The stairwell was painted forest green with orange baseboards and steps so that it looked more like the back stairs of a chain restaurant than an apartment building.

"Do you ever find this to be a bit of a chore?" Harding asked.

"Hmm?"

"Traveling to interview people, I mean."

Graham glanced around and found that they still had one more floor to go. "Would you prefer that we had the power to summon people to the station?"

Harding gave an equivocating tilt of her head. "It'd be more efficient for us," she said.

"Sounds a bit too much like something that might happen in a police state to me," Graham countered. "Ordering people around, when they're not even under suspicion."

Harding thought this through. "I guess it gives us a chance to see where people live," she said. "Their context."

"Precisely," Graham said. "For example, here we are in a modest apartment building in Gorey. What have we already learned before even meeting Miss Miller?"

They were on their way to visit Beth's best friend.

Harding thought, glancing back down the stairs. "We know that she lives in a studio apartment, so it's unlikely that she has a family. The place isn't close enough to the harbor to have a view of the water, and I doubt there'll be a view of the castle either, so the rent will be fairly low."

"Anything else?" Graham asked.

"Parking isn't easy around here, and the building doesn't have its own spaces, so we can guess she doesn't own a car. There's a bus stop outside, though, so she might have chosen the building because she works somewhere beyond Gorey, perhaps St. Helier."

"All reasonable assumptions. Of course," Graham said, "that's all they can be, until we know more." They finally arrived at the right landing and found the door marked 7B. "What kind of job do you think she does?"

Harding puffed out her cheeks. "Could be almost anything."

"Well, there's at least one piece of evidence on that score," Graham reminded her. When Harding's expression remained blank, he tapped his watch theatrically. "Her job allows her to meet with police officers in the middle of a weekday afternoon."

Harding pursed her lips and nodded while Graham knocked on the door.

"You're the detective?" A woman answered.

"Detective Inspector Graham, ma'am. And this is Sergeant Harding."

"Hi, I'm Susan Miller." She extended a hand. "Come on in."

She was exceptionally attractive, Graham noticed, tall and elegant, with long, auburn hair and a figure that suggested many diligent hours in the gym. "Thank you, Miss Miller. As I said on the phone, we're investigating..."

"Beth, yes," Susan said. "I think it's great that you're trying again. Who knows what might come up?"

"That was our thought, too," Graham said, taking the seat offered around her kitchen table. The apartment was small, with a bedroom partitioned from the remainder of the space by curtains printed with an Asian motif. A calming Buddha watched over the room from a large print hanging on the wall as Graham began taking notes. "I wonder what you can tell me about that morning."

Susan poured them all a glass of water, but as she sat down opposite Graham and began to drink, she paused and set hers down. Tears came so quickly. "I waited for her," Susan said, "until I risked being late. I had to run to school in the end. I just couldn't imagine what had happened. It was so unlike her."

Harding used her most consoling tone. "You did nothing wrong, Susan. We're just here to learn more in the hope that we can finally figure out what happened to Beth."

"I just don't know *anything*," she reiterated. "She didn't call or leave me a message on my locker door the day before like she sometimes did. There was nothing. She just didn't show up."

Graham made a note while Harding produced a map of Gorey and asked Susan to point out where she had lived back then. She did so without hesitation.

"You see, that was her house, and here's mine. My house is closer to school. Beth would walk to the corner of my street and wait for me, or I would wait for her."

"How long did it take to get there from her house?" Graham asked her.

"About fifteen minutes," Susan responded, shakily, "we always met at twenty past eight."

"Had she ever been late before?"

"Never," Susan said, drying her eyes. Graham kept up a professional front, but part of him couldn't help regretting that such a beautiful face should be marred by distress. "She was one of the most punctual people I've ever known. We walked together every day for years. And then, she just disappeared into thin air."

"Did anyone pass you as you waited?"

"Of course. Our meeting place was on a main road. I saw lots of people – people going to work, kids like us going to school, even saw a couple of teachers making their way in."

Graham asked Susan the same questions he'd posed Beth's mother. Did Beth have any enemies? Who did she hang out with? Did she have trouble with any of her teachers?

Susan latched onto this last question. "Well, not trouble in the academic sense. She was an excellent student, you know, always on top of her work. Would probably have scored A's across the board if she'd taken her exams." Susan let her emotions resurface for a moment before biting them down again. "But she really didn't like one teacher."

"Who?" Graham asked. But he already knew the answer.

"Mr. Lyon, the science teacher," Susan told him, her voice tight. "He was always assigning her extra work, but..."

She paused, staring down at the tabletop.

"It's okay, Susan. We're speaking in strict confidence today," Harding assured her.

It took a long moment for Susan to gather herself and summon the courage to say what came next. "He and I... we had a relationship," she said almost in a whisper.

Janice waited a moment to see if anything else was forthcoming, then asked, "When was that, love?"

"In the summer before Beth disappeared, before Year 10."

Graham was like a volcano ready to explode. It was all he could do to stay seated. After a pause, he went to make tea in the kitchen, giving the two women time to talk.

"Go on, love," Harding said. "I'm listening."

Susan closed her eyes briefly and took a deep breath. "I managed to convince myself that he was in love with me. I was in love with him."

Susan took another deep breath.

"I would go over to his house during the day and then after school when we went back in September."

It began as a friendship, she told Janice, one that seemed harmless at first. "He was good-looking, much older than me, of course, but nice to me, kind. I was having problems at home, and he seemed genuinely concerned. It was a relief to talk to someone and I felt kind of privileged. I was flattered by his attention, I suppose."

Janice was full of questions, but she knew to let Susan tell the story in her own way.

"And it kind of went on from there. I didn't say no, but I never really said yes, either," she recalled. "He treated me like a girlfriend even though we were never seen together outside his home. I didn't have the heart to refuse him, though I suppose I must have known, deep down, that what we were doing was wrong." She sniffed for a moment, avoiding the officer's gaze, tears in her eyes. "Now I know differently. I can see how naïve I was, how manipulated. I should never have even gone to his house, let alone..." She broke down and needed a long moment to collect herself.

"Did you ever suspect," Graham handed Susan her tea after she had dried her eyes once more, "that there was anything more to his relationship with Beth?"

She sniffed. "I know he was interested in her. I mean, of course he was, she was so pretty, and he paid her a lot of attention. He singled her out, gave her the odd smile. But she never told me about it, if there was."

"And did Beth know about Lyon and you?" Graham asked.

Susan shook her head. "I kept it a secret. He told me it would get him sacked if it ever came out." She burst into tears again. Harding rose to comfort her, and an arm around her shoulders seemed to calm Susan.

"When did your relationship with Lyon end?"

"Erm," Susan dabbed at her eyes, "before Christmas. After Beth disappeared."

Graham and Harding exchanged glances.

Graham completed his notes. "Susan, I understand why you wanted this kept quiet at the time, but ten years have gone by. I wonder if, with the new investigation, you'd like to proceed differently."

"I don't want to do anything," she said definitively. "I don't want to be the victim in all the newspapers and on TV. You *have* to keep me out of it," she insisted.

Harding spoke to her softly. "Susan, this man is a menace. If we can bring one case against him, he might tell us about others. Maybe even," she hazarded, "about Beth."

"You think," Susan said, "that he had something to do with her disappearance?"

"We can't know until we have something solid," Graham told her. "We have uncovered some new leads, but until whoever was responsible tells us what he did with Beth, or we find..."

Susan was shaking her head now. "You're wrong."

"About what, love?" asked Harding.

"There's no way he could have been involved. He wasn't like that." Susan was certain. "It must have been someone else."

Later, emotionally drained and tired, Harding walked slowly down the stairs of the apartment building with Graham.

"That was a lot more intense than I expected," she admitted. "Poor girl. She just couldn't tell anyone what was going on."

"Hmm, it sounds like she thought it all so normal at the time. The one great love."

"More like naïveté, hormones, lack of a stable home life, and the ability to keep a secret. Sir, do you think there's a connection between Beth's disappearance and the ending of their relationship? "

"I don't know," Graham replied grimly, "but now that Susan's told us her secret, we're going to make that count for something. Come on, Sergeant, we've got work to do."

CHAPTER FOURTEEN

I T WAS VERY quiet in the Sanctuary when Roach entered, hoping that the big, heavy, wooden door wouldn't squeak or bang loudly in this silent, echoing place as he closed it behind him. St. Michael's wasn't the smallest church he'd been in, but it had that cozy intimacy familiar to rural houses of worship, especially those with considerable history. The smell that he remembered from his childhood – dust, old books, stonework, and something else that was hard to define assailed him with a wave of memories.

The stone altar was covered with a brilliant, white cloth and adorned only by a gold, bejeweled cross that shone fetchingly in the late-afternoon light through the stained glass windows behind. Two people prayed silently in the front pews. Roach discreetly began to look around for the man he'd been told would be there.

Joe Melton was sweeping the vestry, a small room just off the Sanctuary to the left. His movements were very slow and deliberate. He was of average height but very thin, bearded and gaunt, dressed in old jeans and a checkered shirt.

"Mr. Melton? I'm sorry to disturb you at work."

Joe looked up to see the young police officer in his uniform. "Trouble?" he asked, but carried on with his slow and steady sweeping.

Roach closed the vestry door so that their conversation would remain private. "Just a routine investigation, sir. We're looking into the disappearance of Beth Ridley."

Joe stopped mid-sweep and straightened his back. "Ridley?" he asked.

"Fifteen years old," Roach said, producing a photo of Beth on his phone. "She disappeared ten years ago this week, and we're asking around to see if any new information comes to light."

Melton peered at the digital photo for a long moment. "She was Ann's daughter."

"That's right," Roach answered. "Do you know Mrs. Leach?"

Melton sat down on a hard, wooden chair, wincing at some pain in his back or knees, Roach couldn't tell. "She was kind to me," he said, gazing at the vestry's stone floor. "Good."

Melton was a known transient. An alcoholic, but not a drug user. No convictions or arrests. There weren't even any reports of suspicious activities, something almost unheard of among the homeless community.

"This was when you were sleeping rough, back on Jersey?"

"Aye. Hard times."

"Go on."

"Ann talked to me. Gave me food. Kept me going. I've got demons, you see," he said finally looking up.

Roach took the only other seat in the room, next to the bookshelf. "How do you mean, sir?"

"Drink," Melton answered.

"You seem to be doing well now," Roach offered. It was a half-truth at best. Melton had the face, and in particular the eyes of a man who had been through a great deal. His bent body had clearly weathered storms, and Roach suspected he was suffering from a long-term illness of some kind.

"Passable," Melton qualified. "Haven't had a sip in eight years. Not one."

"Good for you," Roach said genuinely.

"This is the best place for me."

Roach glanced around. "Are you a volunteer here?"

"I live here," Melton said. "Made a deal with the pastor and the church commission. Take care of the place, morning and night. Make sure the kids aren't getting drunk in the churchyard. That kind of thing."

Roach made notes on his tablet. "And what do you remember about Ann's daughter, Beth?"

Melton shrugged. "Saw her walking to school a few times. Wasn't stupid enough to speak to her. Kept my head down. Best to keep a low profile," he added.

"So you wouldn't remember seeing her on her way to school that morning?"

Melton relaxed in his seat. "Ten years ago?" He cracked a smile. "Couldn't have told you what month it was back then. Lived day to day, bottle to bottle. Was all that mattered."

"She used to walk right past the spot where you slept at night," Roach said.

"You think," Melton said, the smile fading, "I spirited her away?"

"We're just trying to trace her movements on that morning."

"Would have been easy enough," Melton said next, raising his chin and scratching his neck thoughtfully as if considering it.

"Easy?"

Melton ignored the question. "Did they find a body?"

"No, sir."

"Pity," was all Melton said.

"How so?" Roach asked.

"Ann will forever think she's alive somewhere," Melton said. He trailed off and seemed to lose interest in their discussion, casting his eyes around the room before standing and resuming his sweeping.

"Do you have any knowledge of what happened to Beth?"

Melton shook his head.

"Where were you, sir, on the morning of Monday November 7th, 2005?" Roach said, suddenly.

"No idea. I told you. Probably sleeping rough somewhere. Probably near Ann's house, like you said."

"Can anyone vouch for that?"

"Course not." Melton hadn't stopped his sweeping.

"Is there anything else you can tell me?"

"Nope."

Feeling defeated after his sudden burst of forthrightness, Roach fought not to telegraph his dejection through his body language. He held out his Gorey Police card.

"I see. Well, that will be all for now, sir," Roach said, his voice tight. "We'll be in touch if we have further questions. And if you remember anything—"

Melton didn't look at Roach. His eyes were fixed on the floor as his brush went back and forth, back and forth.

Roach left the proffered card on the table and departed the vestry without another word.

CHAPTER FIFTEEN

J ANICE HARDING WAS tapping her teeth with a pen, thinking hard. "How about a wildcard search?" she asked. "Add an asterisk to the search term and see what we find?"

"Good plan. Give it a try."

Harding was working with Jack Wentworth, a computer engineer who provided support to the Jersey Police when they faced technological challenges. He had already proved his worth in assisting Janice with the reams of data returned by Andrew Lyon's Internet Service Provider, and now she was engaging him on another issue.

"I'm not sure the online records go back far enough," Jack said. "We're looking for cash transfers or payments to Lyon from about ten years ago, right?"

"Surely they were electronic back then?" Janice asked.

"Some were, but a lot were still manually typed in by a bank teller. Those records are either in an archive somewhere or lost, I'm afraid."

The work was fascinating, if at times a little frustrating. Janice was tasked with tracking down financial transactions between Lyon and the owners of the websites for which he'd done work. It had become part of her personal mission to build a case against the science teacher, and she secretly hoped to uncover evidence of his involvement in Beth Ridley's disappearance.

Working with Wentworth was a bonus. He was an expert in "digital criminality," as he called it, a computer forensics expert. He had had remarkable success in tracking down wrongdoing by those who'd been careless when conducting illicit transactions online. It also didn't hurt from Janice's point of view that he was about her age, good-looking, and single.

"Here," Wentworth pointed out. "There are monthly payments going back at least to 2007 and continuing until the present day."

Janice scrutinized the columns on the spreadsheet in front of her. "Decent amounts, too. They are all a few hundred pounds, at least."

"As payment for what, though?" Wentworth asked rhetorically. "He set up their website years ago. The basic format hasn't changed, just the content, which they can plug into a set of boxes on a traditional web form themselves. Wouldn't even need him to approve it, let alone do new work on it."

The website they were looking at was in the same category as many of the others built by Lyon down the years: technically legal, but morally questionable. It purported to be a "dating exchange," but in reality it had all the hallmarks of an escort service.

"I just can't believe," Harding commented, "that there isn't an actual *crime* in here anywhere."

Wentworth had been impressed from the very beginning with Harding's zeal for her work. He hadn't seen this level of conscientiousness in other police officers he'd worked with. She was absolutely determined to find a way of putting pressure on Lyon. A *lever*, she called it, something she could use to force new information from a man who had been involved with at least one underage girl.

"Writing HTML code isn't a criminal offense," Jack told her. "He did decent work for people who weren't breaking the law. They paid him. The end."

"But there are regular payments to him for no apparent reason."

"Yes, there's that. But so far there's nothing to take to a judge.

"Ah, yes," Harding said. "I wanted to talk to you about that."

Wentworth wondered what was coming next. There seemed no limit to the effort Harding was prepared to put in to bringing Lyon to account.

"Yeah, after our conversation with Susan Miller, we pulled in a few favors. Well, the DI pulled in the favors, and I did the legwork. As a result, I am delighted to be able to give you," she said, reaching into her desk drawer, "*this*."

"Don't tell me," he smiled. "Andrew Lyon's hard drive."

"The very same," Harding said. "The data from his ISP was reason enough to carry out a search and seizure. You should have seen the look on his face when we showed up with the warrant."

Wentworth immediately went to work cataloguing what he had in front of him, then took out an adapter cable he kept in his work satchel.

"Thing is, I doubt there's a smoking gun in there," Harding said. "I mean, unless he's the most complete kind of idiot, he'll have deleted anything to do with Beth."

"If," Wentworth cautioned, "he had anything to do with her disappearance at all."

"Of course."

Janice's initial certainty that Lyon stood at the center of this mystery had been tempered by Susan Miller's strong insistence that Lyon had nothing to do with the case. The thought nagged at her. "People do strange and inexplicable things all the time," she said, mostly to herself.

Wentworth clicked the cable home. "Sounds as though you're familiar with the Jersey dating scene, Sergeant," he quipped. "Alright, the drive is functioning and... Hey, presto!"

Wentworth's laptop screen immediately showed a window listing the drive's contents. "I know you said that he's unlikely to be idiotic enough to leave evidence hanging around for us to find, but I have to tell you, that's often just how it works."

"Really?" Harding asked, shoulder to shoulder with the young man as she read the screen in front of her.

"I helped the St. Helier police nick a guy who had illegally bugged his wife's laptop," Wentworth explained. "He installed spyware, which might sound like nothing, but it breaks the law."

"Sure does," Harding confirmed.

"He was trying to find out if she was having an affair, but when a security scan caught the spyware, and she saw the install date, she called the police on him. They grabbed his hard drive, just like you've done with Mr. Lyon here," Wentworth said, "and do you know what the incriminating folder was called?"

"Enlighten me," Harding smiled.

"'Spying,'" Wentworth said, rolling his eyes. "With

subfolders called 'Gina's Skype Chats' and 'Gina's Emails.' I mean, honestly."

"Honestly," Harding echoed.

"So, some people are not as smart as you think they..." Wentworth's explication of the idiocy of common criminal habits came to a gradual stop as he found something that demanded his attention. "There are over a hundred files in this folder," he said.

"What's the folder called?" Harding asked, peering over Wentworth's shoulder. Then she saw it.

"Beth Ridley."

CHAPTER SIXTEEN

G RAHAM ARRIVED AT the station half an hour early, pulling into his parking space a few minutes before eight. He knew that Janice would not have requested this early meeting unless something of real significance had emerged from her work with Wentworth. The air of excitement around them as they prepared to begin the presentation of their findings was palpable.

"Hang on, you two," Graham said. "I'm a morning man, but only when I've had my second mug of tea." Janice smoothed the process by boiling the kettle while Wentworth double-checked the presentation on the laptop. "Are you going to sell me a timeshare, or is this something about Beth Ridley?" Graham asked.

"Very much the latter, sir," Wentworth assured him.

Once her boss was seated behind his desk, sipping on Earl Grey, Janice launched into her prepared spiel. "Sir, I want to thank you for your help in securing the warrant to seize Lyon's hard drive," she began. "Without it, we'd never have found all of this."

She began to click through a set of slides showing newspaper articles on Beth's disappearance, pages from her school essays, and scans of her school photos, including some that Graham remembered seeing on Ann Leach's living room wall. "We found all of this, unencrypted, on Lyon's hard drive. Right there in a folder labeled with Beth's name."

She continued to show slide after slide of evidence that demonstrated Lyon's obsession with the case.

Graham sipped again. "Go on, Sergeant."

"He kept records of every local and national newspaper report on her disappearance, coverage of events surrounding each anniversary, and even TV news clips relating to the case." Janice clicked to an example, which showed a newsreader recounting the details of Beth's strange vanishing. "He's been studying and archiving the case, sir."

Another sip. "And?"

Janice stared at him. "Well, sir, it's very suspicious. This isn't normal behavior. Why would he be so meticulous about recording a case like this?"

"I'm meticulous about tea, Sergeant," Graham retorted. "And although I often tell you I could murder a cup, it doesn't make me a criminal."

"But, sir," Harding began.

"Say that someone keeps a detailed file on every aspect of the Kennedy assassination. That doesn't tell us that he was the man on the grassy knoll, now does it?" Graham continued.

"Sir, I see what you mean, but don't you find it very suspicious that Lyon would have a collection like this, especially given that he was Beth's teacher... I mean, his collection is *comprehensive*, sir."

"He's still bothered by her disappearance," Graham said. "It occupies his mind. He might even be fixated on it."

"Because he *did* it?" Janice tried. She was still clicking through slides.

Graham stood, walked around his desk and closed the laptop, ending their presentation. "Sergeant Harding, you're a fine police officer. One of the most zealous and committed I've ever worked with."

"Thank you, sir," she said, blushing slightly. She glanced at Wentworth.

"But you're culpable of putting two and two together and getting seven. Fascination doesn't equate to criminality. Obsession doesn't connote murder. And his preoccupation with Beth Ridley shouldn't lead us to assume guilt. What you have here is evidence of "suspicious activity," perhaps a good working definition of "circumstantial evidence," but without something more concrete..."

Janice's face fell. "But think about the ISP results, sir. All those websites, you know, the ones I showed you..."

Graham raised his hands. "He's strange. I don't doubt that for one second. He's got tastes in digital entertainment that are going to get him into trouble. But the reason we don't yet have him under arrest is that we can't charge him. And we can't charge him because we have nothing to charge him *with*."

"I think we could, sir," Harding protested. "The Crown Prosecution Service would probably find the case pretty reasonable and..."

"I simply don't agree, Sergeant. Having questionable predilections doesn't make him a murderer. In the absence of any hard evidence, which this folder unfortunately is *not*, we'd have to hear the words directly *from his own mouth*. It would have to be a full and willing confession."

"Then let's go over there and get one," Harding said, more directly and a good deal more loudly than she'd ever spoken to the DI before. "Let's show him this folder and the ISP records and pressure him into making a statement. Force him to admit what he did."

Graham sighed and returned to his seat. "I could equally go back to Weymouth and arrest the Updikes," he said.

Janice reeled for a second. "But they're just a doddery, old couple."

"According to the criteria you've applied to Lyon, the one-legged doll would more than satisfy the requirements for bringing a criminal case against them," Graham said pointedly. Then he stopped and pulled out his notebook. "That reminds me. Would you two give me a moment, please?"

Harding and Wentworth exchanged a glance and left. Janice closed the door behind them with a decisive click. Graham dialed a number and waited for Dr. Miranda Weiss to pick up.

Dr. Weiss was head of the forensic science lab in Southampton that Jersey Police cases were referred to. She was a tall, sturdy woman in her early fifties, with salt and pepper hair that curled over her shoulders and a penchant for hats that spanned the range from wide-brimmed, formal feather confections to wooly beanies.

An adjunct professor in criminology at the University of Southampton, Miranda Weiss could be stern, but was nevertheless revered by her colleagues and beloved by her students. After thirty years in the profession, her reputation for careful, diligent work that had sent many a criminal to jail was spotless.

"Good morning, Dr. Weiss," he said brightly. "I wonder if you have any news on the doll we submitted to you."

Miranda Weiss was an unabashed coffee addict and was

still in that foggy part of the morning between receiving her first cup of caffeine and actually drinking it. "Yes, indeed I do, Detective Inspector" she began. "But I hope you know how much of a longshot this is."

"I know, Dr. Weiss, but your thoughts would be most helpful," Graham admitted. "A lot of water has gone under the bridge in the last ten years."

"You can say that again," she replied, "So many people must have come into contact with this doll."

Graham sighed. "But we know what we're looking for, don't we?"

Dr. Weiss did not have good news. "Well, not exactly. The hair and fiber samples from Beth Ridley's room were imperfectly stored, I'm afraid, and there's been some deterioration."

Graham swore silently.

"Even if we got a solid hit from DNA on the doll, I don't know if a jury would be convinced. It's been so long. I just wouldn't be able to prove that it was hers, not beyond reasonable doubt."

Dr. Weiss paused to take a sip of her coffee.

"We've got fingerprints from three individuals. You can try running a match, but they're faded and partial. Probably inadmissible. There's also DNA from two females, but that's the most I'll ever be able to tell you about them."

Making notes as usual, Graham asked, "Two females? Definitely no males?"

"You're assuming her abductor was male?" Miranda Weiss asked.

It was both a practical question and something of a challenge to the preconceived notions with which most investigators began missing schoolgirl cases.

"I suppose I was," Graham said, "There's little hard

evidence either way." He dropped his pen resignedly. "Is there any good news, Dr. Weiss?"

"Only for the Updikes," she said. "Reconditioned and fully restored, a doll like this could fetch a pretty penny."

Graham drummed his fingers on his desk.

"I know it isn't what you wanted to hear, Detective Inspector," Miranda said, her voice a little more brisk and confident now that the day's first caffeine was beginning to race around her system, "but the technology only *reveals* the evidence. The information has to *exist* first. We can't invent it. It has to come to us through luck, good judgment, or most often, just painstaking, excellent police work."

It was a timely reminder. "You are right, of course. Thank you, Doctor. I'll run the fingerprints through our database and go from there."

"Any time. Let me know if anything else comes up."

Graham sat at his desk, alone and in silence, for another twenty minutes. Even if the Updikes, with their quirks and strange habits, were actually responsible for Beth's disappearance, the chances of proving it had just shrunk dramatically. But Dr. Weiss was right, the evidence had to be the master of their suppositions. Everything flowed from that.

He strode into Janice's office where she and Jack sat at their computers.

"We can't arrest someone because we *feel* they are suspicious," he said, abruptly picking up the conversation where he'd left off. "Our legal system is the envy of the world, exactly because we presume innocence until guilt is firmly proven."

"Right sir, but..." Harding stopped and frowned, feeling embarrassed. In that moment, made worse by Wentworth's silent presence, she knew that she was being taught another valuable lesson.

"I mean, say that we asked the CPS to read Roach's transcript of his meeting with the homeless man, Joe Melton," Graham continued. "Constable Roach brought up the abduction, and the guy didn't deny it. Said it would have been 'easy' to abduct a girl like Beth. Should we get the Guernsey police to pick him up?"

Staring at her shoes, Janice sighed deeply. "Sorry, sir. Guess I got a bit carried away."

"For all the right reasons," Graham added. "You're focused and passionate, I'll give you that. And you want to nail whoever did this, just like the rest of us. But you're *angry* with Lyon."

"Bloody right I am," Janice growled.

"We know what he did to Susan Miller. We know he works on dodgy websites and has socially unacceptable tastes. We know he's *not a pleasant man.*"

Harding nodded. "But that's all we know, sir."

"Yes." He took a deep breath. "Unfortunately, that's all we know."

"Sorry again, sir." She brushed down her uniform and straightened her jacket. "I let him get to me."

Jack Wentworth who had been sitting stock still, his eyes flicking between the two throughout this tense exchange, cleared his throat. "Sir, we did find something else rather interesting," he said.

Graham ushered them both back into his office and took the opportunity to regard the computer engineer. Wentworth was perhaps five or six years Graham's junior and reminded him of a Hollywood actor whose name he couldn't quite remember. He noted the younger man used gel in his hair. It was spiked up at the front. This was all he needed to underscore their dissimilarity. "You're a civilian, Jack. You get to call me David."

Janice gave her boss a look as though he'd suggested streaking naked through the middle of Gorey.

"David it is then," Jack continued. "Thing is, there are repeated payments to Lyon from at least one Danish website from 2007 right up to the present," he reported. "The website has hardly changed at all during that time, as far as we can tell. Certainly not enough to warrant bringing in a web design professional. If that's not too charitable a description for Mr. Lyon."

"So, what were the payments for?" Graham asked.

"That's what we're trying to find out," Wentworth said. "He must still be providing them with something valuable."

Graham considered this for a moment. "Maybe they're paying him for his silence," Graham wondered aloud. "Maybe the website's really a front for some illegal activity and Lyon demanded regular payoffs to keep quiet about it."

"We'll keep digging," Wentworth promised, and nodded for Janice to lead them both out. "Thanks for your time. I'm sorry this wasn't more of a slam-dunk."

"Oh, they never are," Graham chuckled as Janice and Wentworth turned to leave. "Building a case is more like achieving a maximum break in snooker. You just keep chipping away and chipping away until you get there."

Janice was nodding as she left. Her disappointment was visible, but she knew her boss was right. And, painful though it was, this setback would do absolutely nothing to slow down her pursuit of Andrew Lyon.

CHAPTER SEVENTEEN

CAPTAIN SMITH TAPPED out his pipe on a black-painted stanchion by the marina's railing. "You mean," he said, his gray, bushy eyebrows askew, "like some kind of Special Forces types? Like the ruddy SAS or something?"

Captain Drake, for whom a crackpot theory was always worthy of at least a little enjoyable speculation, set his old friend straight. "All I said was they use *stealth*," he reminded him. "You know. Creeping around at night, and what have you. Dark clothes. Silent movements. That kind of thing."

Barnwell pretended to continue making notes, mainly to mollify these two furious mariners. They could now count five occasions on which their boats had been "boarded and burgled," as Drake put it. There had also been another instance of brazen daylight shoplifting from the nearby store.

"Sorry, Captain Drake, what was that?" Barnwell asked.

"*Stealth*," he said once again. "They sneak around, low and quick, like bloody commandos. That's my theory."

"It's a theory, I'll grant you" Smith commented, "but not a particularly good one."

"Oh yeah?" the other man said, pointing his finger accusingly at Smith. At sixty-seven, Drake thought of the other man as the junior captain, despite both of them having logged an unlikely number of sea miles, many of them in foul conditions. "Let's hear *your* theory, then."

Smith straightened his back. "Common criminals, they are," he said. "But they know just when to strike. It's not *stealth*, it's *intelligence*."

Barnwell narrowly stopped himself from rolling his eyes. "Captains, if we were truly dealing with the gifted master criminals you're imagining, I hardly think they'd spend their evenings raiding Gorey Marina for bits and bobs of nautical equipment."

"Some of it's worth a pretty penny," Drake objected, "if you're selling to the right market."

"He means," Smith pointed out to his friend, "that if they were like the crooks from that film... *Ocean's Eleven*, that's it, they'd be stealing the sodding Crown Jewels or some such, not ruddy bits of rope and nautical charts."

"Hang the bloomin' Crown Jewels," Drake growled. "What are you going to *do* about all of this?" He pointed at Barnwell, his temper was up.

"Well, that's what I'm here to talk to you about," Barnwell told them.

He explained for a few moments, hoping that his news would come across as the well-considered plan it truly was. Barnwell had been working hard. He had dragooned two extra officers from St. Helier to help patrol the marina at night and had consulted with an expert at the Metropolitan Police in London who had arranged to loan Gorey a set of sophisticated detection devices.

"Motion sensors?" Drake asked, examining the small, black, rectangular box with its three protruding antennae.

"*Anything* that moves down here," Barnwell explained, gesturing across the marina, "right down to the size of a house cat, this baby will pick it up."

"Then what?" Smith said, rather nonplussed.

"It triggers a high-definition camera system that we're going to mount on the sea wall and on three of the boats. They'll all be connected, and they'll all go off at once, taking a set of pictures that will give us a complete view of the Marina."

Drake handled the camera as though it might explode. "Fancy," he announced. "But what about *below* the waterline?"

Smith exploded in a gale of laughter. "Christ alive, what now?" he guffawed. "You think these thieves are gonna approach by submarine like Seal Team Six?"

"I'm just saying..." Drake tried, but Smith waved him down, crumpling with laughter.

Barnwell hid a smirk and pressed on. "I've also asked the boating supplies shop to re-task its brand new CCTV cameras to scan the marina at night. With two lines for potential photographic evidence, we should have a good shot at identifying the thieves."

Smith recovered sufficiently to give Barnwell a clap on the back. "Well, fella, you've thought this through, I can tell. I just hope you get some results."

Barnwell left the pair and began setting up the camera system. He was proud of his plan and hopeful it would bear fruit. With luck, he'd soon have stand-up-in-court photos of the perpetrators. With a little more, he'd personally catch them red-handed.

CHAPTER EIGHTEEN

F ROM HER SMALL office at the station, Janice was distracted from her work as she listened to Constable Roach making another phone call in the reception area. She sat up straight and made a conscious effort to focus on her screen. Jack was due in a few moments, and they had more work to do. She wanted to be prepared so they could hit the ground running as soon as he arrived.

Their topic of research was a new one. With Lyon's illicit past laid bare, but without any hard evidence, and with DI Graham still apparently chewing on how best to proceed, Harding had suggested that she and Wentworth investigate a different area: The Beth Ridley Foundation. She wanted to do some digging and see what, or who, they turned up.

"Okay, Sergeant," Graham had said when she'd suggested it, "a little due diligence would be in order. You might look at all the people connected with it – organizers, supporters, donors, even the investigators they've hired. It's possible that Beth's abductor is hanging around among that lot."

"Surely not, sir."

"You'd be surprised. Wouldn't be the first criminal to stick around and get his jollies from witnessing the chaos he created," the DI had warned.

All of this, happily enough for Janice, kept Jack around for at least one more day. She enjoyed working with him and was happy to give up her Saturday if it meant gaining the benefit of his expertise.

"Damn."

Janice pulled herself away from her computer once again and popped her head around the office door. "Everything alright, Jim?"

He was still holding the phone receiver. "I really thought I had something there," Roach said, almost to himself. "Damn it all."

Janice put things together quickly. "Joe Melton?"

"The very same," Roach said. He was still staring at the phone, perhaps in the hopes it would ring and he'd hear a different kind of news.

"Still a potential suspect?" Janice asked.

"Nope."

"Ah."

"Owing to the remarkably good recordkeeping of our local hospital, we are now able to say categorically that Joe Melton was not responsible for the abduction of Beth Ridley. He was admitted with 'chest pains,' Roach explained, "and eventually treated for mild hypothermia and dehydration. He had a night in a comfortable bed, and then returned to wandering around Gorey, sleeping in the bushes, and drinking himself stupid. He was discharged the same day Beth disappeared, but not until the middle of the afternoon."

"So, he's off our list," Janice summed up. "Bugger, indeed."

Roach looked at her. "You know, there was something about him. I *wanted* it to be him. I *wanted* that possibility, so I could track it down, prove it, and make everyone see that he wasn't some reformed drunk, but rather a monster."

Roach had a pleading look in his eyes now, which was soon met with a fluster of self-doubt. "That's not a great way to think about a criminal case, is it?"

Janice took a seat in the otherwise empty reception area. "It's not, Jim, but I understand it."

Roach was crestfallen. His only solid contribution to the case had evaporated. Beth's journal continued to make only partial sense, and it hurt him, almost physically, that Beth's abductor, whether it was Lyon or someone else, remained free.

"But, you know," Janice continued, "our job is all about the *truth*. Uncovering it, describing it, and proving it. We can *want* a certain outcome as much and as deeply as we like, but in the end, only the truth matters."

Roach propped both elbows on the reception desk. "You want it to be Lyon, don't you?"

Janice nodded. "I'm *aching* for him to stand there in front of a judge and be handed some long sentence. I've found myself daydreaming about it."

"Understandable," Roach commented.

"Sure, but it's still *wrong*," Janice cautioned. "We've both been fixated on the *person* and not on the *evidence*."

It was Roach's turn to nod. "You're getting wiser by the day, Sergeant Harding, if I may say so."

"You may. Reckon it's down to that brainbox who runs this place," she smiled, heading back to her office again. Then she paused and approached the desk, speaking in hushed tones. "Do you know what our illustrious leader did the other day?"

"What?" Roach said, happy to distract himself with a little office gossip.

"I showed him a list of websites... I don't know, maybe thirty or forty of them, all different and all with pretty complicated names. Some were just a string of numbers and letters. Made no sense to me at all."

"Yeah?" Roach said.

"He *memorized* that list, Jim. All forty addresses. I couldn't have shown it to him for more than a minute. He remembered the whole lot."

Roach nodded, smiling. "Impressive. Probably really handy in the field, too.

"I shouldn't wonder. I mean, he's a bit of a marvel, isn't he?" Janice said.

"And how are you getting on with Jack?" Roach tried to keep a teasing tone out of his voice.

"Great! He's been so helpful. He's going to do a complete forensic investigation on Lyon's hard disk. Do you know they can find proof of files existing even after they've been deleted? He's a bit of a marvel, too."

From right behind her came a familiar voice. "Well, I don't know about that, but I'm willing to agree with you if you force me to."

Roach greeted the new arrival brightly. "Morning, Jack! Welcome to a sunny Saturday at the Gorey Constabulary."

"I'm missing the big game right now, you know. Fourth round cup tie," Jack said. "But I guess Saturday pays time-and-a-half, so there's that."

Janice, who had been shuffling papers on a desk finally

turned, gave him a smile, and gestured to her office. "Morning. Shall we get started?" As she shepherded Jack to her door, she shot Roach a glance. He shrugged, grinned at her, and returned to a stack of filing he'd been putting off for days.

"So," Jack said, setting down his satchel and taking his usual seat behind her desk. "I've actually made a start already," he explained. "Did a bit of digging through the electronic records last night."

Janice couldn't resist. "Didn't you have anything better to do on a Friday night, Jack?"

He didn't take the bait. "Oh, I love a bit of sleuthing. Makes me feel like I've wandered into a crime novel."

Roach appeared at the door. "Sorry, Sergeant, but could I bother you for a copy of that list you were talking about?"

"The websites?" she asked, with a glance at Wentworth. "There's some pretty hot stuff in there, Jim. You sure you can handle it?"

"I'll manage," he said, hands on hips.

"Go ahead and print it off the Jersey Police mainframe," she said. "It's in the Ridley investigation directory. Lyon folder."

"Well," Janice said, returning her attention to Wentworth, "what did you find?"

Jack opened his laptop and showed her a summary, just under a page long. "The Beth Ridley Foundation," he said simply, "is an open-and-shut case of fraud."

"Bloody hell." Graham re-read Wentworth's printout of the document for the third time. "How come no one knew about this?"

"There's been a crackdown on charities, sir," Jack said.

Jack had been struggling to heed Graham's request to use his first name. Like everyone else, he couldn't shake the automatic deference Graham's presence elicited.

"But they've been focusing on ones likely to be laundering money for terrorists or drug cartels, that kind of thing. Foundations of this size tend to slip under the radar. Besides, it couldn't help but look insensitive. Ann Leach is on the foundation's committee. Their mission is to help find her missing daughter, after all."

"Yes, indeed," Graham said, handing him back the document, "but that's *not* what they've been doing, is it?"

Janice shook her head. "So far, I've found at least three different ways in which Beth's mother has rerouted funds from the charity to a small network of shell companies that she directly owns."

"Amazing," Graham allowed. "Just goes to show, doesn't it? She plays the grieving mother like an Oscar-winner, and not the brightest bulb at that, but all the time, she's been conniving and fiddling the books with the best of them."

Wentworth glanced at his notes again. "Not *all* the time, sir. The fraud seems to have begun about three years after Beth went missing. Before that, the private investigations, lab tests, all the rest of it, they were genuine. But after that point, an increasing number of the expenditures were bogus. Now, nearly all of them are."

Graham poured himself yet another cup of tea. It was more out of habit than any urgent need for caffeine. Jack and Janice had called him away from a pleasant afternoon at the library reading up on Jersey's local history, but under the circumstances, he didn't mind a bit.

His initial surprise at Ann's deceit was giving way to a determination that they must build the best possible case.

"It won't do for us to charge the mother of a missing girl and then have it dismissed on some technicality. This has to be absolutely watertight."

"Right, sir," Janice agreed.

Graham paused for a moment, thinking. "Any sniff of a suspect behind this smoke and mirrors act?"

"Doesn't look like it, sir."

"Hmm, okay then. I want you to bring this in for a landing. Build the case, interview people, get whatever help you need within reason. Jack here, for instance. He's been very helpful, wouldn't you say?"

Janice gave Graham an especially careful nod. "Yes, sir. He's an expert in this stuff."

"You're too kind," Jack said with a smile.

"Great. Work on it together, and then liaise with the CPS to make sure all our ducks are in a row before we make the arrest. I'd love a couple of co-conspirators as well, if you can manage it. Look into siblings, accountants, and those who gave large amounts to the charity."

Janice made quick and detailed notes. "You're thinking that they took the tax breaks for charitable donations, but then got a nice kickback from Ann?"

Graham shrugged. "It's what I'd do, if I were giving to a charity I knew was crooked. Look into it, and keep me posted."

CHAPTER NINETEEN

J IM ROACH MADE a second pot of coffee and
then returned to his screen. He'd been up since five
and at the station since six, unable to settle into his
normal Sunday routine of fitness training, lunch
down the pub, and maybe an old movie on BBC2. The case
was bothering him on many levels, not least his own
inability to meaningfully contribute to it.

He was poring over Beth's journals once more,
desperate to make meaning of her teenage musings. As he
carefully turned the page, the pencil in his hand skimming
the edge of the paper, he suddenly paused. He backed up
and read over the looped, girlish handwriting on the
previous page. As his thoughts swirled, he looked around,
tapping his pencil.

He turned back to the journal again and flipped a few
pages ahead. Backward and forward he turned the leaves of
the book, making notes on a yellow legal pad as he checked
details. His excitement was mounting. Finally, he reached
for the phone.

"DI Graham? Yes, I know it's Sunday, sir... Well,

thanks. Erm, is there any way you could come to the station, sir?"

DI Graham burst through the doors of the small police station like an explosion.

"This better be good, Constable. This is the second day and the second weekend in a row I've been called in. I was in the middle of one of Mrs. Taylor's overwhelming but utterly delicious breakfasts."

"I'm really sorry about that, sir. But I think this is important."

"Oh?"

"I saw something in Beth's journal that went *click* in my brain."

"Show me," Graham said.

Roach pointed to his own notes from their interview with Andrew Lyon.

"He said he was a heavy smoker. And it connects with something Beth wrote about Cat in her journal. That he stank."

Graham took seconds to make the connection. "So, you think Lyon is this Cat person, and the smell she referred to was cigarette smoke?"

"Yes, sir. She talks about him all the way through the journal. Always in rather childish language, as you can see," Roach said, flipping through some pages he'd bookmarked with yellow tabs, "but it's beyond dispute who she's talking about. And, you know, '*Lyon*', sir," He emphasized the name.

DI Graham raised his eyebrows, and turned his head very slightly to look at Roach.

"As in 'king of the jungle,' sir."

"Ah."

Graham went into his office and sat alone, reading the journal carefully over the next ten minutes. He reappeared looking determined. Angry, even. "Right, that's it. I know we're waiting to have a cast iron case against Lyon for doing *something* to Beth Ridley, but we can needle him on the Internet stuff, and if Susan Miller will agree to contribute anonymously to the trial, nail him on at least one set of underage abuse charges."

Roach nodded, "Okay, sir. So, what now?"

"We bring him in," Graham's jaw jutted out. "We stop mucking around. I want him in an interview room, under arrest, so we can sweat him for forty-eight hours. Come on. Let's go nab him before he sees the writing on the wall and spends his ill-gotten porn money on a flight to a non-extradition country!"

Graham sat opposite Andrew Lyon and his lawyer, Mr. Sutton, in the station's small interview room.

"Do you understand these charges as they have been read to you?" Graham asked Lyon after reading the sheet out loud.

Harding had produced a long list of offenses, but Graham knew that without further evidence, he'd be hard-pressed to make most of them stick.

The pale, now rather crumpled ex-teacher nodded. For the most part, he'd been staring at the green tiled floor or the freshly-painted white walls. Anywhere but at Graham.

"For the tape, I can verify that Mr. Lyon nodded his assent." This wasn't the first time in the hours-long interview that Graham had been obliged to report Lyon's responses for the record. Sutton was making sure he said as little as possible.

Graham knew the lawyer to be seasoned; one who worked hard for his clients, and someone with experience defending others on similar serious charges in the past.

"I remind you once more that my client has the right to remain silent," Sutton said. He had a haughty, reedy voice, like a private school tutor from a hundred years ago. "We'll be filing a request that the charges are dismissed on technical and procedural grounds."

Graham had been expecting something of this nature.

"We believe that your seizure of Mr. Lyon's personal possessions are in contradiction of legal directives regarding the privacy of information," Sutton announced, officiously.

"Such a filing is your prerogative," Graham said.

"Is there anything more you would like to say, Mr. Lyon?"

There wasn't. Graham stood to leave.

"Mr. Sutton, it would be in your client's interests to begin cooperating with us. I have a strong suspicion that the list of charges against him is only set to grow." With that, he left Sutton to advise Lyon further and went in search of tea in the reception area.

CHAPTER TWENTY

"FRESH POT BREWING, sir," Roach told him.

"Top man, Constable." Graham leaned against the desk with a sigh. He looked tired; interviews during which the suspect said absolutely nothing were wearing.

"How's it going in there, sir?" the young officer asked.

"Sutton's making sure that the little bugger is staying as silent as a monk. But we'll get to him, don't you worry."

"Right, sir," Roach said.

Sergeant Harding appeared in reception, shaking out her umbrella. "Just started pouring down!" she told them, and then she set a plastic bag full of takeout on the reception desk. "Chicken jalfrezi with extra chilies, lamb curry, poppadums, and naan bread. That'll be seven pounds each, please." Roach and Graham fumbled for change in their pockets while Harding peered through the peephole of the interview room door. "That blasted lawyer's still here? Has Lyon said anything?"

"Silent as a church mouse," Roach told her as he opened

the takeout box of outrageously spicy Indian food. "And looking to stay that way."

Graham ignored his meal for the moment. He paced the lobby, walking past the notice board with its posters about community events, firework safety, and the best ways to deter burglars.

"Constable Roach, Sergeant Harding... Would you step into my office? Bring your food."

"Everything alright, sir?" Roach asked.

"We need to mull this whole thing over in peace. We'll leave the door open in case anyone comes in to reception."

Janice and Roach followed their boss and took seats in Graham's office.

"Okay, so we've been looking at three suspects, basically," Graham began. He went to the small whiteboard on the far wall. "The Updikes, Joe Melton, and Andrew Lyon," he said, writing the three names alongside each other.

"Melton's not our guy," Roach reported. "Like I said, the hospital records..."

"Yeah," Graham said, crossing out the name. "The timing doesn't fit. Then there's the old couple."

"They had the broken doll in their possession," Janice said.

Graham wagged the pen at her. "They had *a* broken doll in their possession, Sergeant, and sadly, but not unexpectedly, we did not get a match for Beth's DNA or fingerprints from it. Two and two make four, and no more than that."

"But we matched the manufacturer," Roach argued. "It was the same type as the doll Beth was carrying on the morning she vanished. It *could* be the exact same one."

Graham put a large question mark next to the Updikes'

name. "It *could* be, but it's certainly not going to work in court as it stands. We'd need firm evidence..."

"Of which there is precisely sod all," Janice noted with frustration.

"...Or a cast iron witness," Graham added.

"Of which there are none," Roach concluded.

"So, the Updikes are out, too?" Janice asked. The smell of curry was making her distinctly hungry, and she began to wish she'd ordered something for herself.

"There's just no motive," Graham said, "no reason for a quiet, old couple to grab a teenager off the street and make her vanish. I mean, they're a bit odd..."

"A *bit*?" Roach interjected. "Their most prized possession in all the world was a plate signed by a chef from a royal wedding thirty odd years ago."

"Being a bit quirky," Graham retorted, "doesn't make one a murderer. I mean, we've all got our vices, but that's all they are. For the most part."

"Alright," Janice said, her stomach growling. "So, speaking of vices and whether or not they're harmless, we're back to our old friend, Mr. Lyon. Can we really pin this on him?"

"Susan Miller says no," Graham said. "She insisted that Lyon isn't the type."

Roach scoffed at this. "I'm sure she'd have sworn blind that he wasn't the type to mess around with schoolgirls until he started doing exactly that," he said. "Neither was he the type to work for a Danish porn site, until..."

"Point is," Graham interrupted, "we still don't have any concrete evidence linking him to an abduction or even Internet wrongdoing, if we're honest."

"Well," Janice said, still frustrated, "she didn't abduct herself."

"No," Graham agreed. "Unless, I mean..."

Roach spotted the line of thought. "She did a runner?"

"On her own?" Janice said, picking up the thread. "Without money, or a passport, or credit cards?"

Roach frowned. "You have to admit, sir, it's the least likely explanation. What about her mother?"

"Ah," Graham said, readily moving on, "Yes."

The case against Ann Leach had been developing steadily, and Graham was now certain they could justify bringing her in for questioning. "We're police officers, not politicians," Graham said, "but we have to be aware of the gigantic fuss we'll create in this community if we arrest Ann Leach."

Janice nodded. "She's received a lot of sympathy and accepted so many donations over a long period of time. I've no idea what the public will make of an arrest."

"Or what they'll do," Roach added. "They might turn on her."

"Or us," Janice added.

"It's a risk, certainly" Graham said. "But do you think she had anything to do with Beth's disappearance?"

"Maybe Beth didn't get along too well with Ann's second husband," Janice suggested. "You know how teenagers are... Big changes tend to bring heightened emotions, with lots of yelling and crying. Don't forget that Beth's biological father was sent down for murder."

Janice visualized the scene.

"Her father gets sent to jail on the mainland, her mother immediately divorces him, and then there's some new guy in the picture. Must have been traumatic, especially for a young girl. She's stuck in the background, seething with resentment and hostility."

Graham drew a spidery set of lines on the board,

connecting these different points. Seeing it laid out like this was often a help to him, but so far, nothing was falling into place.

"We can only imagine how Beth responded, how difficult she might have made things for Ann," Janice added.

Graham looked at her oddly. "So, Ann decides one morning to abduct her own daughter, just so she can have a nice, quiet life with her new man?"

Janice shrugged. "We're throwing theories around, and that's a theory," she said. "Perhaps they were in cahoots together. Beth wanted out, Ann enabled her disappearance, and spun the story as a way to commit fraud."

Graham looked her doubtfully. "Okay, maybe not, but I'll say this, sir," she continued, "I've been doing this job long enough to know that, well, people are *weird*. They do *weird* things that defy explanation. I'm just saying."

Graham opened his takeout and began eating. "They do, Sergeant. For sure."

While Graham and Harding were back in the interview room, attempting to wring information from Lyon, Roach made sure that no one entered the station while his back was turned. Given the nature of his research, he was most grateful that his workstation wasn't visible from the station's lobby. A desperate member of the public staggering in for help and finding the desk constable surfing through dozens of Danish websites, many of them questionable, would not be a good PR or a wise career move.

Some of the websites he was surfing were found in the colorful and rather incriminating browser history of Andrew Lyon. Others were owned by companies for which

Lyon had done web design work. Most of them featured women in various stages of undress.

There were redheads and brunettes, even a smattering of Asian and African women, but the majority were blonds, mostly with clearly eastern European backgrounds. He lost count of the number of women named "Anna" or "Katya," though some went by professional names – "Jewel," "Sunshine," and "Glitter" among them. They were bright, upbeat names for those involved, whether entirely willingly or not, in a decidedly dark and seedy business.

He browsed through portrait shots of dozens upon dozens of women, briefly reading what he guessed were their largely fictional biographies. Every half hour or so, when his eyes began to blur and ache from the constant stream of images, he stood and stretched before reading another section of the Beth Ridley case file. Every interview and lead was chronicled there, and he'd built a comprehensive picture of what his colleagues had already investigated.

When Roach had directly exhausted the list of sites for which Lyon had done work, he began rather aimlessly clicking links to their affiliates. He brought up a gaudy affair with a host of flashing banners and looping animations on fast repeat.

The site boasted that it had over two hundred of the "hottest girls in Europe." He shivered slightly and then moved onto another site. This time the presentation and tone were quite different. Whether legitimate or not, the website design was tasteful and restrained. None of the women advertising here were overtly offering libidinous experiences. Some specialized in massage or other forms of therapy.

"Yeah, right," Roach muttered to himself. "I bet, in real life, they don't look anything like their..."

He stopped and doubled back.

"Wait a minute."

Roach peered at the screen and then clicked on the photo to enlarge it.

"Wait a cotton pickin' minute."

He downloaded the picture, zoomed in, and printed it out in three different resolutions. A visitor to the station would now have found him staring at three identical pictures of the same woman, laid out on the reception desk.

He toyed with the idea of knocking on the interview room door when it abruptly opened and the DI appeared.

"Sir? You need to see this. I think I've got something."

CHAPTER TWENTY-ONE

"BETTINA," GRAHAM ANNOUNCED, reading the woman's one-paragraph biography.

"Might not be her real name," Roach advised.

Graham nodded. "Hardly ever is, right?" He returned to the description. "'This twenty-five year old is an educated blond who specializes in...'" He read on for a moment. "*Blah-blah-blah*, this and that, services and therapies... All euphemisms, I'd imagine. But this one's clearly captured your attention, Constable. Want to tell me why?"

Roach stood up straight. This was his moment, and although his theory was certain to be controversial, perhaps even instantly rubbished by his colleagues, he was going to state it and then stand by it. He'd never felt more certain in his life.

"That's Beth Ridley, sir."

Graham looked at Roach with something approaching shock, then back at the picture, and then back to Roach. "Son, that's one hell of a... Are you sure?"

"Yes, sir."

Graham stared at the pictures again. He leaned over the

desk, picked up the case file that Roach had been looking through, and took out Beth's school photo. He put it next to the ones taken from the website, his eyes flicking rapidly between them.

"I know it's a shock, sir... But hear me out," Roach pressed.

Graham stopped him. "Get Sergeant Harding. Have her pick up Susan Miller. We need more eyes on this."

"Should we bring in her mother?"

"No. Not yet."

"Righto, sir." Roach went to pull Janice out of the interview room. Within moments, she was on her way.

"And, Constable?" Graham said, still looking at the photographs.

"Sir?"

"If it turns out you're right about this, I'm going to make sure the whole world of British policing knows that it came from you."

Once again, Graham felt it prudent to shift the discussion about the photographs into his own office. He was very keen not to let the cat out of the bag. Part of him was, in fact, still rather uncertain as to whether the metaphorical bag genuinely contained the requisite cat.

"She's the right age," Roach reminded him as they waited for Sergeant Harding to return to the station with Susan Miller. "Twenty-five, give or take, right?"

Graham decided that it was best to play Devil's Advocate. He wanted to guard against jumping to conclusions. Susan would confirm Roach's suspicions if they were well-placed.

"Half the girls on that website are in the right age range, Constable. Probably more than that."

"Okay," Roach admitted. "But her eyes, sir. They're quite distinctive." Roach showed him a copy of the last portrait from Ann Leach's living room wall, and Graham was reminded just how amazingly blue Beth's eyes were, like a pair of sapphires, gleaming out from the photo as she smiled for the camera.

"But not unique," Graham cautioned.

Roach sighed and walked back to the reception desk. It seemed that his boss was determined to rain on his parade, and just when he had finally begun to harbor some hope.

The front doors opened and Janice arrived with a rather worried-looking Susan Miller in tow. They made their way to Graham's office, passing Roach on the way. He caught Susan's eye and nodded awkwardly, mindful of their mutual past and her recently revealed secret. From his work on Beth's journal, he suspected Susan Miller was "Mouse."

Graham extended a hand. "Very good of you to come in, Miss Miller. Especially on a Sunday and at short notice."

Susan seemed on edge. Janice looked at her carefully. She understood the truth behind those worried looks. She knew Susan wanted to help find Beth but was desperate to avoid any public revelations about her past. Janice showed the younger woman to Graham's office and had her sit down. She brought her a glass of water.

"We're working on an image of Beth as she might appear now," Graham said to Susan. Janice looked on as her boss worked through the narrative he'd composed earlier. It was aimed at ensuring secrecy. "It's so difficult to extrapolate facial features over a period of ten years," he explained, "so we're asking people who knew her well whether or not they'd find the image convincing."

Roach had carefully cropped the photo so that only Beth's face and hair were visible. Graham showed it to Susan and asked, "How do you think we did?"

Susan picked up the image, her lips pursed. She scrutinized it closely, clearly searching for particular details. "It's..." she began, then glanced at Graham and Janice in turn before returning to the picture. "It's *uncanny*."

"Really?" Graham said, feigning pride to conceal the immense rush of adrenalin he suddenly felt. "You're not just being kind?"

"Absolutely uncanny," Susan repeated. "Her eyes... The shape of her nose... You've captured her perfectly."

"Well, that's great news," Graham told Susan. "You've made my day, I'll be honest. Thank you."

Graham raised his eyes to Harding.

Get her home. We've got work to do.

CHAPTER TWENTY-TWO

R OB AND CHARLIE waited until sunset to make their final preparations. Rob quietly brought out a stash of equipment from the lean-to they'd roughly constructed from an old door and a couple of sturdy planks. Charlie set about stowing them onboard. They worked on the boat in silence, following a careful plan agreed upon long before.

Charlie was particularly proud of the boat itself. The *Sea Witch* was a sturdy fishing vessel, probably sixty years old. The original idea to restore it had been Rob's, and together they drew up plans to patch the leaky hull, install new equipment, and work to make the old girl seaworthy again. If only for this one vital expedition.

The *Witch* sat on a makeshift boat ramp at the bottom of the garden. Charlie's family home backed on to the beach, and the carefully tended lawn close to the house gave way to coarse, reed-like grass and then sand. At high tide, they could launch the boat directly into the water.

Most of the boat's hull was obscured from the house, certainly from anyone looking out of the kitchen windows, but much of it was visible from the house's upstairs bedrooms. This didn't bother Rob or Charlie too much. Those in the house knew they were reconditioning the boat and had seen the change in its color as the two applied new coats of paint. It was all fine just as long as those in the house never found out the real mission behind their restoration project.

Rob brought out the third box of equipment. The two would-be sailors began finalizing stowage and proper mountings for the gear. There was a powerful lamp that Charlie screwed to an existing metal mounting outside the pilot house. Rob then attached the GPS to the battered wood of the console.

"Jesus," Charlie observed as he came back into the boat's pilot house. "Couldn't you have managed to put the bloody thing on straight? It's as crooked as a mafia lawyer, man."

Rob pushed annoying strands of ginger hair from his eyes and offered Charlie the screwdriver. "Have a go yourself, then. This wood has been warping for longer than we've been alive. I'm amazed it didn't splinter into pieces when I drove the screw in."

"Alright," Charlie conceded. "Just provided we're all stowed and ready to go in four hours."

"Ready or not," Rob reminded him, "that's when we go. No more waiting around. It's high tide, and it's high time."

Charlie agreed. "Dunno why we waited this long, honestly. Come and help me with the last lot, alright?"

These were the heaviest items yet; a pair of storage boxes that weighed enough to have them both heaving and complaining as they were shoved aboard and stowed under some tarpaulin.

Once they were secure, Charlie flexed his tired shoulders and then turned to his friend thoughtfully. "You nervous?"

"About tonight?" Rob asked.

"Our first time out in her," Charlie reminded him. "Might be dangerous."

Rob took his friend by both shoulders. "It'll be worth it. Imagine the upside, eh?"

"Right," Charlie agreed. "I just wanna be sure we're doing the right thing."

Rob gave a short laugh. "Course we are, mate. This time tomorrow, all our problems will be over." He gave Charlie a wink. "Trust me. Tonight at ten, alright? We'll aim for the deep water and put some miles between us and trouble. It'll all go fine."

"Sure it will," Charlie agreed. "This time tomorrow, eh?"

Graham approached Roach at the reception desk.

"Well, sir?" Roach asked anxiously. "What did Susan say?"

Graham wanted to clap the young man on the back and buy him a slap-up dinner at the Bangkok Palace. But he knew that there were still hurdles to overcome and that they carried the burden of proof.

"You might be onto something," he said simply.

"Bloody hell," Roach breathed.

Graham turned to head back into his office but stopped and approached the reception desk. "I meant to commend you for sleuthing out the nicknames in Beth's journal," he said quietly. "But I couldn't help noticing that 'Bug' remains unidentified."

"Yes, sir," Roach said. "It's been difficult to piece together the—"

"Constable?" Graham said, yet more quietly.

"Sir?"

"You do know that I sniff out lies, cover-ups, and deception for a living, right?" Graham put to him.

"Lies, sir?" Roach said, his heart thumping. "I don't think I..."

"It can't have been easy, seeing your own nickname in her journal after all these years and in these circumstances," Graham added delicately. "I can only imagine the turmoil you've been going through."

Roach swallowed and then closed his eyes for a moment. "I didn't want you taking me off the case, sir. You know, for loss of objectivity, or because you couldn't trust my judgment."

"Jim, you're becoming a very able officer, and I'd have wanted you as part of this case, no matter what," Graham said. "You knew her. You've been the only one to make sense of her journal. And now your diligence and persistence have given us a hot new lead. I can't think of a more valuable resource than you right now."

"Thank you, sir. I'd do anything to help get to the bottom of this," Roach said. Harding waited patiently at a distance for Graham to finish this rather mysterious, private conversation with his subordinate.

"But mark this, Constable Roach. If you've got evidence, I want to see it. I don't care if it's inconvenient, troubling, or emotionally draining. In fact," Graham continued with a slight smile, "I don't care if it shows that my old Granny Graham was a ninja assassin. Don't hide things from me, son. We'll always be able to work it out. I want you to trust that. Alright?"

Roach met the DI's gaze. He was grateful beyond words, but he was going through a curious mix of sensations: relief, embarrassment, regret, admiration for his boss, and an ongoing determination not to let *anything* get in the way of this investigation.

"Alright, sir. Thank you. Honestly."

"'Honestly' is the only way I want it, son. Keep doing what you're doing. And in the meantime, Constable Roach," Graham said much more loudly, for Harding's benefit, "you'd better see about organizing some plane tickets for the two of us. Leaving early tomorrow, if you can," he added.

"To where, sir?" Roach asked, suddenly much more excited.

"Denmark, of course."

Later that evening with Janice off home and Barnwell out pounding the beat in and around the streets of Gorey, Roach knocked on Graham's office door. The DI waved him in. Their flights were booked and plans for the trip to Copenhagen had been laid.

Roach sniffed the air. "It smells like a curry house in here, sir."

"Occupational hazard, Constable. What can I do you for?"

Roach raised an eyebrow. "Constable Barnwell's on the phone, sir. There's been a sighting of an unregistered boat acting suspiciously just offshore."

"Unregistered?" Graham asked through a mouthful of leftover naan bread. "How common is that around here?"

"Not in the slightest, sir. The local sailors and fishermen

all know to have their paperwork in order. He reckons something sketchy is going on. The lifeboat's been called out but he wants permission to get the Coast Guard helicopter from the mainland."

Graham rose. "Put him through. I'll talk to him. I don't doubt his judgment, but I'd like a few more details before we do something expensive. It'll take an hour to get a chopper here, anyway." He thought for a second. "What's the boat's name?"

Roach reached for his notepad once more. "The *Sea Witch,* sir."

CHAPTER TWENTY-THREE

CHARLIE GRINNED CONSTANTLY as the boat made steady progress across surprisingly calm waters. Illuminated by the boat's two powerful lamps and the light of a waxing moon, the English Channel looked inviting and easily navigable, absent the foamy, terrifying swells that would have made this journey impossible. Their luck, so far at least, was definitely in.

"Twelve knots," Charlie observed as Rob clunked the heavy door of the pilot house closed, returning from a quick look outside. It was only half a dozen degrees above freezing tonight, but the pilot house was warm, thanks to a small space heater that ran off the old boat's creaking power system.

"How many knots did you say?" Rob asked him.

"Twelve!" Charlie repeated proudly.

"Christ, I never thought the old girl would have it in her. How much cruising time, do you think?"

Charlie checked their GPS and a nautical chart they'd brought as backup. Neither of them was prepared to say how long the electrical system might hold up. "Should be there in about two or three hours," Charlie announced. "Two AM or a little after, unless we hit trouble."

"We'll be fine," Rob assured him. He patted the wood of the pilot house interior. "She's got more miles left in her than anyone would guess."

The *Sea Witch* had something of a checkered history. Almost broken up for scrap in the early 1970s, the twenty-four foot vessel had come into the possession of Charlie's grandfather, who had done a creditable repair job and put the *Witch* to sea as a day-fishing boat. He'd spent most weekends for a few years puttering around the coast of Jersey, but he became notorious locally for his inability to ever actually catch anything.

This notoriety peaked, when on returning home one dark evening, he'd steered the small boat onto submerged rocks. The *Witch* limped home, its sole crewman required to constantly bail out a worrying amount of seawater. He'd made a decent job of repairing the boat, but within weeks of lowering its patched-up hull back into the water, Charlie's grandfather had been diagnosed with lung cancer and was gone within the year.

After his death, the boat was hauled onto a ramp and effectively forgotten about, becoming a strange, light-blue relic fossilizing at the bottom of the family garden until Charlie and Rob, propelled by their plan, made it an evening restoration project. They had worked often well into the night, sometimes through the night, but no one ever suspected that the boat might actually float, let alone achieve a princely twelve knots. Now, the *Witch* was on her most daring adventure. One that had to remain absolutely secret.

"Say that again, would you, Constable? It's ruddy noisy where you are."

Barnwell stepped away from the roar of the Caterpillar diesel engine that was warming up. "Sorry, sir. They're saying it's an old boat that was registered years ago but not since. Reckoned it had sunk or was scuppered somewhere."

Graham thought quickly. "So, what's the idea? That someone is using an unregistered boat to commit a crime?"

Barnwell stepped further away as the lifeboat's second diesel lit up. He raised his voice further.

"I'm not sure, sir. But I'll tell you my first thought, if you'll allow some speculation."

"Go for it," Graham told him, reaching for a pen.

"Is there any reason we can think of," Barnwell said, "why someone might be moving an object from land to sea, at this particular moment in time?"

Graham was silent for a moment. "What are you think-ing, son?"

"That case, sir. The one you've all been talking about in the office. Beth Ridley. I mean, sir," Barnwell continued, the noise behind him becoming fierce, "that if time were of the essence, perhaps because of an ongoing police investigation, then it might be a rather neat way to dispose of *evidence*, sir."

Finally, it dawned on Graham what Barnwell was suggesting, and he grinned at the new-found investigative prowess of his constable. "Is this where our two investiga-tions find a meeting point, Barnwell?"

"Like I say, sir, it's just speculation. But if I knew the location of evidence relating to the Beth Ridley case, and knew that my fingerprints or DNA were all over them, I'd certainly consider asking a friend to dump them in the Channel for me."

"Interesting conjecture, Constable. Whether you're right or not, get the lifeboat out there, and tell them not to spare the horses. Or, whatever you say when you need a boat to get a serious move on."

"Yes, sir." *Click.*

Graham put the phone down, looked from Harding to Roach and back again. Then he marched straight to the interview room and flung open the door.

"Detective Inspector..." Sutton began, rising in complaint.

"Lyon, I'm going to ask you this straight. If you answer me in a comprehensive fashion, I might try to persuade the judge from handing down the most horrific of jail sentences."

Sutton blustered, "My client has already asserted his right to remain..."

"Lyon, listen to me," Graham said, staring hard at the pale, terrified man. "Do you have friends who are at sea tonight?"

Lyon blinked a few times, then shook his head.

"The *Sea Witch.* A knackered, old fishing boat. They're out there, right now. Did *you* hire them?" Graham demanded.

Lyon looked at Graham for almost the first time since his arrest. "I have no idea what you're talking about," he said quietly.

"Think carefully now, Mr. Lyon," Graham continued. "Because if we intercept that boat and find something incriminating, you'll spend the rest of your life in the darkest, most horrible hole in the entire United Kingdom, I personally guarantee you of that."

"Andrew, I must remind you," Sutton began once more, "that everything you say in here is part of the record..."

"I have nothing to say," Lyon said, finally.

The image presented itself to Graham of Lyon's bruised, battered face, a horrified Sutton screaming at Graham to stop, and Janice Harding dashing into the room to pull her boss off the whimpering, bleeding Andrew Lyon.

Calm down, Graham warned himself.

Janice appeared at the doorway. "Could you come to the phone, sir?" she asked gingerly.

Graham took a long moment to pull himself away from the table. Part of him still wanted to make Lyon bleed. At length, he straightened up, turned away, and headed to the phone, barely in control of his emotions. Another image flashed into his mind: that of his two year-old daughter sitting in her high chair as he blew soapy bubbles over her head, laughing as she tried to catch them, squinting as they burst on her nose. He pushed the image away.

"Graham," he said distractedly into the receiver.

"Sir, it's Barnwell again." The background noise was different now, a rhythmic sloshing as the *George Sullivan* made its way across the nighttime waves.

"Yes, Constable?" the DI replied, his mind still very much elsewhere.

"I've got something on that boat. You remember I put in a report about some shoplifting from the store by the marina?"

Graham's mind swam slowly back to the present moment. "Shoplifting?" he asked.

"Paint, sir. That special stuff they use on boats, to stop the hulls from..."

"Yes, I remember," he said. "A few days ago. What of it?"

His boss sounded stressed, so Barnwell cut to the chase. "The description of the boat we're chasing. The *color* of the paint, sir. It's the same color as that on the hull of the *Sea Witch*.

"I'm not *following* you, son," Graham said tersely.

"Sir, the two men who did the shoplifting that day... The men I chased from the marina... This boat. I think they are connected."

"What?" Graham said.

"The marina thieves, sir," Barnwell said. "*They're* the crew of the *Sea Witch*. They've been nicking gear for weeks. Radar, GPS, maps, paint, all the things you'd need to re-fit an old boat and then navigate to a point only they know where."

"Navigate?" Graham said, the cogs of his mind only just beginning to revolve usefully again. "Navigate *where*? And *why*?"

"I don't know, sir, but we're on their tail. We'll find out."

CHAPTER TWENTY-FOUR

THE SOUND ARRIVED unexpectedly, and it was as dreadful as it was worrying.

"Jesus, Mary, and Joseph," Charlie spluttered. The steady droning of the engine, which had been a reassuring bass line throughout their journey, was interrupted by a horrendous, metallic clanging, as though an elementary school percussion ensemble had taken delivery of a large bag of hammers.

"Shut it off!" Rob yelled. Charlie's hands were already at the engine controls, throttling back the ancient diesel and allowing it to stall. "What the hell, man?"

A plume of black smoke arose from the diesel engines, illuminated now by two powerful lamps that Charlie turned toward the stern. He swore colorfully.

"Okay, okay. We can fix it, right? We've got the tool box, haven't we?"

They did indeed, but in the dark and with the engine still scorching hot, it would not be an easy task.

Fifteen minutes later, sweating, angry, and in pain from

the scorch marks he'd picked up from brushing against hot metal, Rob stood up.

"Try her again," he cried to Charlie, who was at the controls. Charlie turned the engine over. Nothing. Rob threw down his screwdriver, "Godammit!"

Charlie came outside, and the pair stared at the motor as though demanding that it explain itself. Rob walked to the bow of the small fishing boat. "Let's face it, Charlie," he finally said. "It's over. Time to call for help."

Charlie stared at Rob, then lurched forward grabbing his friend by the collar of his waterproofs. "Are you serious? What are we going to do? We have too much riding on this to give up now! How the bloody hell are we going to explain what we are doing out here, eh?"

Rob shrugged. "We tell them the truth."

Charlie snorted. "Oh, great! Terrific! That's just *vintage* Robbie, that is. Absolutely classic. Let's call up the Coast Guard and tell them everything. Maybe ask them to bring the police, too! Make a *real* party of it!" Charlie gestured wildly at the dark sky. "Maybe just ask them to take us straight to jail and be done with it. Why bother messing around with a trial? Do not pass 'Go,' do not collect two hundred pounds, just end up banged up for theft and God knows what else..."

Rob stared impassively in the face of Charlie's tantrum. "We have no choice unless we want to die out here."

Charlie took another breath, ready to continue, but the look on his friend's face stopped him. The breath left him in a long sigh of resignation. "Sorry, Rob, lad. I didn't mean all that, mate. I'm just, you know, with the...We'll get *crucified*."

"I know. But it's over, Charlie." Rob sighed. "Let's radio for help." As he turned there was a sloshing sound at his feet. The two youths looked down and then at each other in alarm.

The boat was taking on water.

Sergeant Janice Harding remained determined to project an air of professionalism throughout this trying night, but she couldn't help enjoying the *Schadenfreude* that came from locking a cell door on Andrew Lyon.

"Now, you just keep quiet like a good boy," she chided, "and once DI Graham is free again, I'm sure he'll have you brought up for further questioning." She had already deprived Lyon of his belt, and their recently-installed CCTV system would free her to observe Lyon's incarceration from the reception area.

She returned there to join Roach, who was helping liaise with the lifeboat dispatcher at St. Helier. The Coast Guard helicopter from Lee-On-Solent was on standby in case of trouble, and the dispatcher told them that there was even a Royal Navy warship that could be there in ninety minutes, complete with a helicopter full of heavily armed Royal Marines, if necessary. Janice didn't anticipate they would be required, but it was clear that whoever was piloting the *Sea Witch* for whatever reason, was in for a very rough night.

The phone rang. Janice listened for a few seconds and started taking notes.

"Right, ma'am. I'll send someone out to you as soon as we can...Yes, ma'am...We will...Thank you... Yes."

As soon as she put the phone down, she turned to Roach.

"Guess what? Report of a stolen boat." She ripped off a

page from her notebook and handed it to Roach. "Get yourself down there, lad. Might be the one Barnwell is chasing. Let us know what you find out."

"But, Sarge, I was just about to go home, I've got to be on a plane in a few hours."

"Sorry, Roachie, but this is what real policing's all about. All hands on deck and that." She smiled at her own little witticism as Roach slapped on his police cap and made his way outside.

With Janice manning the phones and radio and Constable Roach dispatched to check out the missing boat report, Graham found himself with little more to do than speculate on what on earth might happen next.

"What if it's Ann Leach making a run for it?" Janice put forth. "You know, she got wind that we're about to pull the plug on her charity and decided to do a runner with the rest of the money."

Graham regarded her with a mix of skepticism and obvious amusement. "Sergeant, if you ever tire of police work, you might try your hand at writing mystery novels."

"You're too kind, sir."

"Besides," Graham added, "how could she know that we've discovered so much about her financial situation?" When Janice shrugged, Graham raised a finger, his eyes wide. "Aha! Jack Wentworth! He's secretly playing for both sides!"

Janice blushed a little. "Leave Jack out of it, sir. He's doing no such thing."

Graham's serious demeanor gradually returned. "I mean, it could be a lot more innocent. Just two idiots taking a boat out for a joyride."

"At night?" Janice pointed out.

"Sure," Graham replied. "Nice and quiet, a bit of fresh air..."

"In winter?" she said next.

It was Graham's turn to shrug. "Alright. People traffickers, how about that? You know, those gangs who bring in migrants for exorbitant fees. They've got a boat load of refugees, and they're trying to make it to the mainland."

"Via Jersey?" Harding said.

Graham thought quickly. "Just for a refueling stop."

"What about drug-running?" Harding asked.

"Oh, good one," Graham said. Then he paused for a moment. "Has there been much of that around here?"

Before Janice could answer, the phone went again. Graham picked it up, glad for something to do.

"Roach." Graham listened for a moment. "You're where? Shelton Avenue?" And then he groaned. "Hodgson."

Janice recognized the name. "The lad who's always wandering off at night? Is he missing again?" she asked.

Graham listened for another minute, thanked the Constable, and replaced the receiver. "Well, I'll be a monkey's uncle. Charlie Hodgson and his mate, Rob Boyle are missing, along with their boat."

"My father used to swear he'd put a lock on the *outside* of my bedroom door if I..." Janice began, but noticed that her boss was deep in thought. "Sir?"

He looked up at her. "There's bad news, and there's bad news."

"Bad news first, please," Janice said.

"Our theory about intercepting the imminent disposal of the remaining Beth Ridley evidence and wrapping the case up beyond a shadow of a doubt appears to have fallen apart," he said. "There's no way that these two are involved in something like that. They're seventeen and barely have a functioning brain cell between them."

Janice breathed a loud and sincere sigh of disappointment.

"And the other bad news?"

"They have about as much seafaring experience as I have."

"How much is that, sir?"

"None."

CHAPTER TWENTY-FIVE

"RIGHTO, SIR, I'LL tell them," Barnwell said into the radio. He had earlier ruefully considered that after all his high tech efforts down at the marina, it was a simple sighting by a fisherman setting up for an early start the next day that had set them on the trail of the rogue boat. Now his hopes of solving the Beth Ridley case had come to naught, too. It just didn't seem fair.

The lifeboat crew consisted of volunteer, well-trained mariners with the Royal National Lifeboat Institute, whose mission was to help those in distress around the British coastline. They had been called out by the Jersey Coast Guard. It was too dark and windy for the spotter plane to be of any use, and the mainland helicopter was too far away.

"Understood," Will Ryan, the captain of the lifeboat said after Barnwell explained what he'd learned from Graham about the identities of the two they were chasing. "I'm not a gambling man," Ryan explained, "but I'd wager a bottle of scotch that the *Sea Witch* is not having a good time. From your description, it sounds like she should have stayed on her boat ramp. I just hope we get there in time."

Ryan imagined their troubles while scratching a bushy, brown beard that his wife had once described as "enthusiastic."

The *George Sullivan*, named after the lifeboat's designer, ploughed handily through the waves, keeping up a brisk but not yet nausea-inducing twenty-six knots. She was a capable, 53-foot vessel, in the unmistakable orange of the RNLI, with two powerful diesel engines. The crew were seasoned, dedicated volunteers, all holding down jobs on the mainland that allowed them to be called out at any time of the day or night to rescue those who got into trouble out in the cold, coastal water.

The *George Sullivan's* radar scanned the horizon ahead while a crewman broadcast a repeated message over the emergency channels, requesting the *Sea Witch* respond and cut its engines. So far, there had been no reply.

Barnwell answered his radio once more and then relayed another message to the captain. "One of the young men on the *Sea Witch* has a very irate mother. She'd prefer that we pick him up and bring him home, but 'only if it's not too much trouble,'" Barnwell reported.

"Someone's in for an earful," a crewman observed.

"If he's not drowned himself by now," Barnwell pointed out.

There came a loud, clear call from the lookout positioned on the lifeboat's railing. "*Light ho!*"

Captain Ryan followed the lookout's pointing arm, and saw a tiny glimmer on the horizon. "Good eye, man! Hang on, everyone." The lifeboat lurched as Ryan demanded full power from her twin diesel engines. With a surge of noise and power, the *George Sullivan* rocketed over the waves toward the light, while her radar confirmed that this was a small, seafaring craft and not one of the big container vessels that routinely passed through the channel.

"*Sea Witch, Sea Witch,* this is the *George Sullivan,* are you receiving me, over?"

The only reply was static.

"*Sea Witch,* approaching from your northeast. Please cut your engine and signal with a flare."

"I wouldn't be too hopeful," Ryan said. "If they're daft enough to put to sea in a rusted wreck..."

"Actually," Barnwell felt it fair to say, "they nicked a box of flares the other week. And life jackets, for that matter."

The lifeboat's captain gave him a very strange look. "Just what kind of people are these?" he asked, mystified.

"Teenagers," Barnwell replied simply.

"Ah."

"*Sea Witch, Sea Witch,* this is the *George Sullivan.* We are to your northeast, five hundred yards and closing. Please signal."

Moments later, as the lifeboat's powerful main light found the cobalt blue vessel, the reason for the lack of reply became obvious. "Oh, hell," Ryan muttered. "She's down at the bow."

Barnwell struggled to view the scene through the front windows. The lifeboat's spotlight caused extraordinary glare, and he could barely make out anything amid the choppy waves. "What does that mean?" he asked, blinking at the sudden brightness.

"She's bloody well sinking," Ryan reported, "just like I warned you. She won't be above water for much longer. Pete, get on the loudhailer. The crew, for want of a better word, must be around here somewhere. Names?"

"Uh... Barnwell thought for a moment, "Charlie and Rob."

Pete grabbed the ship's bullhorn and headed outside to the railing. Barnwell heard the call, which would have been audible a mile away. "Charlie? Rob? This is the RNLI. Shout if you can hear me!" Pete's day job as a Phys Ed teacher at the high school in St. Helier gave his raised voice an insistent clarity that was impossible to ignore.

Barnwell's radio crackled. "Constable?" He cursed under his breath. Barnwell had promised Graham updates every ten minutes, and he was long overdue.

"Yes, sir. Sorry. We've arrived at the location of the *Sea Witch*, but she's taken on a lot of water. There's no sign of the boys."

Barnwell heard the DI swearing on the radio. "I wish we could do more to help you, son," Graham finally said. "Is there no sign of them at all?"

"Not at the moment, sir, but we're on it. I'll give you an update shortly."

Captain Ryan ordered the boat's engines to be cut, the better to hear faint yells across the water. "Start a search pattern with the light," he ordered. "Focus to the landward of the wreck."

"Why is that?" Barnwell asked. His best recourse, he knew, was to simply stay out of the way, but he also hoped to be helpful.

"Because, nine times out of ten, people moving away from a sinking ship will head in the direction of land, even if it's miles away." Ryan was as anxious for news as he was angry at the two young idiots who had risked their lives in a hopeless vessel. "Why the hell didn't they get a distress call out?"

"Maybe their radio broke," Barnwell offered.

"Well, I'll be very glad to be wrong, Constable, but at the moment it looks as though you and I are going to be delivering some bad news later tonight," Ryan said, thudding the console with a curled fist. "And I bloody well *hate* it, when we lose people out here. And for no reason at all! It's not as though we're trying to get a convoy past the U-boats or navigating through a sodding hurricane. I mean, we're six miles off *Jersey*."

The island was off to their right, little more than a long, thin band of distant lights now.

Pete kept calling as the whole crew silently waited for a response, scanning the seas around them for a sighting of the lads. "Come on, you silly buggers," Barnwell muttered to himself. "Come *on*..."

The light swept back and forth, searching the area north of the sinking boat. "There!" Pete shouted.

Barnwell was at the rail before he knew it. "Where?"

Pete was gesturing with a straight arm. "Three points off port."

That meant little to Barnwell until he saw movement within the cone of light thrown by the big lamp.

"Jesus," he breathed. "Charlie? Rob? Can you hear us!" he called out, as loud as he could.

"Here!" they heard. It was a faint, tense, panicked sound. "Over here!"

The spotlight had picked up Rob, his head and shoulders bobbing above water buoyed by his stolen life jacket.

"Can you see the other one?" Ryan demanded, now ordering the lifeboat's engines to minimal power and steering her toward the flailing teenager.

"Rudder amidships and prepare to cut engines."

As they approached, the *Sea Witch* began her final dive, her silent engines briefly facing the sky as the boat nose-dived to the bottom.

"Okay, cut it now." The lifeboat's diesel engine died

once more, and Pete tossed a rope to Rob, who immediately grabbed for it. "Good lad! We're pulling you in."

Ryan was becoming more and more agitated. "Where's the *other one*?" he growled. "Get that searchlight moving again!"

It was Barnwell who saw Charlie Hodgson first. "There!" he shouted. "Christ, he's drifted away. Get the..." But before Barnwell could even find the right nautical words, he found himself taking off his shoes and jacket.

"Oi, wait, we've got a..." he heard Pete saying behind him. But Barnwell slung a leg over the railing, took a deep breath, and jumped feet first into the English Channel.

The water was shockingly, unbearably cold. Barnwell surfaced hurriedly and roared out an oath worthy of a seasoned sailor and then swam hard in Charlie's direction. The ship's light had found the boy now, an incongruous, linear shape in this world of watery curves. He was resting high in the water, his orange life vest inflated, but he was facing away from Barnwell. And he wasn't moving.

Barnwell heard splashes to his left as a rope was tossed into the water. He reached for Charlie's life vest and spun the boy around.

Charlie lolled in the water, unconscious. His eyes were half-closed, only the whites visible. He was ghostly pale. "It's okay, lad. I've got you." Barnwell slid the rope around Charlie's chest, and locked it in place. He signaled to the boat that had come in as close as it could.

Swiftly, the immobile teenager was dragged through the freezing water and pulled to safety. One member of the lifeboat crew immediately began chest compressions while the other prepared to winch Barnwell in.

Another rope was thrown to Barnwell. He grabbed it with frozen hands and locked it around his chest but as he turned and began to swim, he felt a strong tug as his line went taut before it slackened as the locking mechanism gave way. The rope was gone, splashing uselessly across the surface ahead of him.

"Bugger!" He tried to grab it, but he was losing the feeling in his arms. The cold was now seeping deep into him. Barnwell grasped at the surface, trying to push the water down and away, but it always rose again, shoving icy water in his face, chilling him down to the bone.

Dazed, he saw a hazy, fading figure at the rail of the lifeboat. Something flew into the air, but he hadn't the strength to follow it. His legs felt unbearably heavy, his soaked clothes acting as anchors and dragging him down. He found that he was all but motionless, hovering above a chasm of freezing darkness that was pulling at him, insisting, demanding, tugging harder and harder...

Slap.

It was sudden, rude, and harsh.

"Again," came a voice.

Slap.

"Oi!" Barnwell grumbled indistinctly. "Wossat all about, then?"

Slap.

"Stop!" he finally roared, his eyes blinking open as he raised himself up, only to find his progress impeded by four strong hands.

"Take it easy, Constable." It was Pete and another crewman whose name he hadn't learned. "You're going to be fine."

"Where am..." But he heard the sounds at once; the

noise of the diesel motors, the waves sliding under the hull and lapping at the sides of the *George Sullivan*. Then came warm applause from the lifeboat crew.

"Welcome back, son," Will Ryan said, handing Barnwell a big mug of steaming hot coffee. "Drink this. Slowly," he warned.

Barnwell sat up on the comfortably padded stretcher that he had been laid on. Next to him were Rob and Charlie, pale and silent but conscious. Lifeboatman Pete helped to keep the thermal blanket wrapped around his chest and shoulders as the wet, chilled Constable reached out to take the mug. Though his features felt like they were chiseled from a block of ice, he managed a grin of gratitude. "Thanks, Captain."

The older man chuckled. "I hope you're not a teetotaler or anything, 'cos there's an enormous tot of navy rum in there."

Barnwell noticed the aroma immediately, and it seemed to warm his whole being. "Just this once," he said, taking a cautious sip and finding the coffee to be sweet, strong, and excellent, "I think we'll be alright."

CHAPTER TWENTY-SIX

THEY WERE STANDING in front of the converted industrial buildings that were now home to many of Christiania's inhabitants, a four-story, weather-beaten place with plenty of greenery planted outside. A couple of dogs were asleep in its shade.

"Can't say I've ever been anywhere quite like this before," Roach admitted.

"Can't say I have, either," Graham said. "Probably because this place is unique in all the world."

Christiania, they'd found out via the Internet the evening before, was a self-administered commune, right in the center of Denmark's capital city. Its independence was protected by the state, and the commune enjoyed the freedom to decide some of its own laws. This, as the two officers had instantly noticed upon arriving, included the legal and public consumption of marijuana.

"Can we, you know," Roach asked a little awkwardly, "get a bit high from just being here?"

"Why do you ask, Constable?" Graham replied with a

slight smile. He checked his phone once more. "Are we completely sure this is the right building?"

"I'm pretty sure this time," said Roach.

Graham had instructed Roach not to wear a uniform or any insignia today, leaving him feeling odd and slightly naked. They were well outside of their jurisdiction, and Graham was keen to carry out this most delicate part of the investigation without unnecessary fuss. In this part of the city more than any other, uniforms would attract unwelcome attention and suspicion.

After working all through Sunday and into the early hours of Monday morning confirming that Constable Barnwell and the two teens were safe, Graham and Roach boarded a plane to London and from there another to Copenhagen. Both of them dozed off on each leg of the trip.

They awoke for the final time as the second aircraft landed smoothly in what was a considerably wet and dreary Copenhagen. Feeling as dreadful as the weather, they caught a taxi into the city center and immediately decamped to a local café. There they found the buttery, sweet pastries and steaming, strong coffee overcame their fatigue as they strategized the next part of their mission.

Roach had been in favor of informing their Danish counterparts of their visits and told Graham so during the previous evening. Graham had overruled him, and by the time they landed, he had persuaded Roach of the virtues of a more clandestine approach.

"If it really is Beth," Graham had reminded the younger officer, "we've got no idea what her status is in Denmark. She might be staying here illegally, or with people who are wanted by the police, or she may even be wanted herself for all we know. If we show up with uniformed Danish cops, she might run, and then we'll never find her again."

Graham rang the intercom button for apartment 452, and only then realized that he had no idea what he was going to say if anyone replied. He blinked for a moment, thinking rapidly.

"*Hvem der?*"

Graham cleared his throat. "Er, yes. I'm here to visit Bettina," Graham said. "Erm. We're, erm..." *Get it together, Dave, for heaven's sake.* "I called this morning?"

He'd called an automated service organized through her website, which let him leave a voicemail message. She had responded with a short email.

"The Englishman?" the voice asked. Bettina spoke without a distinctive Danish accent.

"Yes, that's right. I made an appointment."

The silence that followed grew so long that it became agonizing. Graham glanced at Roach, who was hopping nervously from foot to foot. In the café, Roach had suggested that he might simply reveal himself to be her old classmate, but Graham had scotched that idea, too. His objection wasn't specific. They just couldn't predict even slightly how she might react to being identified after so long. Instead, Graham had pretended to be a potential client. Bettina had advertised herself as an aromatherapist and reiki healer.

Graham reached for the intercom button again. Then, "Come in." *Buzz.*

Graham made a sudden decision, "Constable, I'm going in alone. If you hear nothing from me in thirty minutes, ring the doorbell. If no one answers, call the local police. It's 114 on your phone. Then call Harding. Got it?"

"Got it," Roach replied. He watched his boss enter the building and walk up the first flight of stairs and around a corner.

The place needed a lick of paint, but Graham had been inside the bolt-holes of runaway teenagers and other dislocated types plenty of times, and they'd been far worse than this. The apartment block had a neglected, slightly foreboding feel. He didn't pass a soul.

Short hallways branched off each landing, leading to groups of four apartments on each side. A black cat glared at him as he rounded the corner onto the third-floor landing. The cat shot down the hallway as if to warn someone. Graham shivered and wished once more that it had been possible to bring some kind of weapon, even a can of pepper spray. He also wondered how anyone could run much of a business from a place such as this.

There it was, apartment 452. He knocked softly and waited.

The door opened, its chain still in place. "I'm sorry, I thought the appointment was for later. I'm not quite ready." she said through the gap. Bettina was a tall, attractive woman. Graham guessed she was in her mid-twenties. The right age. Ocean blue eyes. Her hair, though, was an audacious experiment, a kaleidoscope of purple-blue-green-red that formed a psychedelic spiral around her face.

"I can come in and wait." Graham had wondered whether a casual or a formal tone would sound better, and ended up lapsing into his usual, deferential politeness.

"Alright," she said resignedly, and the chain slid back. "But, like I said, nothing's ready."

"That's really not a problem."

The apartment was neat, airy, and well-kept. Plants adorned every shelf in the kitchen, where there were dozens of cookbooks and a surrealist sculpture of the Eiffel tower, swollen and deranged but oddly transfixing. Off the kitchen was a bedroom, its door mostly closed. Opposite the small kitchen island sat a thoroughly beaten-up leather sofa and some bean bags. If he didn't know better, he'd have taken it for a shared student apartment.

"Sit here for a moment while I set up my therapy room." The woman looked over toward another door, completely closed this time, to the right of the bedroom.

"Erm, no, please," Graham demurred, "Could we just talk for a moment?"

"I'll just—"

"No, really."

She looked at Graham quizzically, considering him, then walked to a tall barstool at the kitchen island and gestured for him to sit on a second one. She reached for a half-consumed joint that lay in a thick, glass ashtray.

"So?" she asked, "What do you want to talk to me about?" She lit up and now regarded Graham with a genuine curiosity. He didn't look like a regular customer. He was too straight-laced, too "establishment." If anything came across in those first moments with this tall British visitor, it was *loneliness*. "You know, most of the people who come here are pregnant women and their boyfriends," she said.

"They are?" Graham asked, wondering how he was going to begin.

"Yeah, you know. People who are looking for a different way to relax. I use aromatherapy and the power of touch, sometimes crystals, to restore balance and sweep away stress in the body."

Graham smiled slightly. "We could all use a little of that, I suppose."

"Were you looking for something in particular?" she asked. Her deep, blue eyes were pleasant and welcoming, the kind he normally associated with peace-loving hippies and mind-blown festival-goers. There was nothing in them that spoke of trauma or loss. He cringed inwardly at the thought that he might still, after all of this, be speaking to entirely the wrong woman.

"I've actually just come from Jersey," he began.

Bettina puffed out a cloud of smoke. "Oh, yeah?"

Graham watched for any signs of recognition, but she was either hiding her reaction or had never given the Bailiwick any thought. He plowed on.

"I've been there for a few months, and recently I was asked to investigate something that happened there a few years ago."

Now she paused. He was certain he saw it. A little hiatus in the way she lifted the joint to her lips. "Investigate?" she asked.

"Yes, there was an anniversary, recently," Graham explained, "of the day a local girl went missing. A schoolgirl, only fifteen years old."

Bettina took another puff but said nothing. Her eyes left Graham and roamed the room. She had begun to look just a little on edge.

"No one had any idea what happened to her," Graham continued. "Her mother has been searching, all these years," he added, very aware of the risk in bringing Ann up so early in this complex interview and choosing not to use her name. "And other people too, her friends and family, everyone's just desperate to know what happened to her."

The woman stubbed out the joint carefully. "And have you found out?" she asked as she watched the smoke rise in a final grey curl.

"I think I'm beginning to understand what happened, yes," Graham said. "But I was wondering if you might be able to help me."

She was breathing faster now.

"Help you?" she asked. "In what way? How has any of that to do with me?"

Graham took a breath. He was too far in to back out now.

"Because I believe you to be Elizabeth Ridley, formerly of Gorey, Jersey who disappeared on Monday November 7th, 2005."

CHAPTER TWENTY-SEVEN

S HE LOOKED AT him squarely. "Don't be ridiculous. I am Bettina Nisted. I grew up in Aarhus. I moved to Copenhagen three years ago."

"I don't believe that's true," Graham replied. She was cool, he'd give her that.

"Of course, it is."

Graham raised an eyebrow but said nothing for a moment.

"Miss Nisted, facial recognition software and age progression imaging techniques, as well as testing on various biometrics such as fingerprints, your ears, or the irises of your eyes, will prove beyond a doubt whether you are Beth or Bettina," Graham said, his gaze level, watching her reactions closely. "But they are expensive techniques, and they take time. Besides, I suspect your mother would know you at a glance. It would be better if you'd simply tell me the truth." He paused, but seeing no reaction from the woman in front of him, he continued, "Perhaps you can tell me why you came here."

She stood suddenly, the stool skidding away from under

her with a metallic shriek. "*Came* here?" she said loudly. "You think I *chose* to come here of my own free will?"

Graham was caught in a whirlwind of emotion, but as the furious woman stood there before him, red-faced now with anger, the sensation he felt most keenly was one of the very sweetest relief.

He stood then, both palms face down as he sought to calm her, "Beth, I know you didn't choose to come here."

"Don't call me that," she spat.

"I'm sorry. Bettina. I've been investigating what happened to you."

"You shouldn't have come here." She reached into her pocket for her phone. "You're going to get me into trouble."

"Andrew Lyon is at my police station in a holding cell," he said.

Everything stopped. Her hands were still. She couldn't take her eyes off Graham now. "A *cell*?" she asked. She was silent for a moment, and Graham wondered if she was picturing the scene. "You're the police?"

Graham brought out his wallet and showed her his ID. "Detective Inspector David Graham of the Gorey Constabulary," he said.

"Gorey," she said, as if finding the word in her mind for the first time in many years. "You're from Gorey?"

"I head the local police unit there," Graham explained.

"And... You've arrested him? Cat?"

"Yes," Graham confirmed. "We have him, and we're not going to let him go. We just didn't understand what had happened to you and... well, with no evidence, we feared the very worst."

Her expression changed yet again. "Well, I'm alive. But nobody can know I'm here," she said resolutely. "You *mustn't* tell *anyone*." The final words came out in a hiss.

Graham held up his hands. "Absolutely. It's your right, and I'll abide by whatever you say."

She stared for a moment assessing him, then sat back down, and took a deep breath. "Does my mother know?"

"No," Graham said quickly. "You can tell her if you want to. But she doesn't know we're here or even that we're following a lead that you might still be alive."

The young woman pursed her lips and wrapped her arms around her waist.

Graham felt as though he were treading on deep wounds that were covered with shards of glass, any slight misstep threatening to not only re-open old injuries, but also to cut them deeper. "Your mother gave us access to your old journal. She thought it might be helpful."

"My journal?" she said, as though she hadn't thought about it in years.

"Beth, we've been carrying out two investigations. One was into Andrew Lyon's past and his use of the Internet. He's in a lot of trouble."

This time, she didn't react to his use of her name.

"He should die for what he did to Susan," she said simply. She saw Graham's look of surprise.

"Oh, she thought I didn't know, but I did. You should help him hang himself or something."

Graham moved swiftly on. "And then, I'm afraid, we've had to take a closer look at the charity your mother has been running."

"I saw something about it. All those investigators and researchers. I was afraid they might find me." She paused. "She's been stealing, hasn't she?"

He blinked for a second before telling her, "Yes, it looks very much as though she has."

"Typical."

"How so?" Graham asked.

Beth snorted derisively. "Because she's a liar and a cheat, and she never thinks about anyone except herself. I knew that Gorey, my mother, and Lyon weren't going to just vanish. But I wish they would."

CHAPTER TWENTY-EIGHT

BETH STARED OUT of the window. The view beyond was horizontally dissected by the faux wood blinds. "I did hope Lyon might die before I ever heard his name again," she said.

She didn't sound malicious. It was more as though she were convinced that the universe, in its own sweet time, would discover and punish Andrew Lyon for all he had done.

"An investigation is ongoing," Graham told her, "but try as we might, Lyon hasn't been persuaded to tell us anything about you. Or about his relationship with Susan Miller."

There was another dismissive, unimpressed snort. "*Relationship*? Oh, please. It wasn't roses and candles, you know. He didn't wine and dine her. He groomed her, made her trust him. I guess she told you the rest."

"Yes, but she won't testify against him," Graham pointed out.

"I'm not surprised. The media, everyone in Gorey, the whole of Jersey would be all over her, and it's the last thing she deserves.

"I need to ask you something, but please take your time," Graham began.

"How did I come to be in Denmark?"

"Yes."

Graham brought out his notebook, his mind filled with equal measures of curiosity and dread.

"One minute, I was on my way to school, trying to decide if I had time to drop my doll off for repair. The next, I was blindfolded and in the back of a van being driven somewhere."

Graham's gut knotted. "What then?"

"A day or so later, I'm not sure, the door opened, and I was pulled out into a muddy field. There was a conversation in a language I didn't understand, and then I was shoved in another car and driven to a house in the countryside. Training, they called it, at first. Then "work." she said simply. "Lots of threats, lots of men, lots of foreign languages. They never hit me, but they used drugs and coercion, and they told me lie after lie. I didn't know which way was up."

She sighed.

"I can't remember a lot of it. Blocked it, I suppose. I prefer to focus on my future."

Graham leaned forward, his elbow leaning on the island, his hands clasped. "I appreciate you telling me this," he said quietly.

"Oh, I've been through it all before," she said, matter-of-factly.

Graham blinked.

"With the Danish police. Seven years ago, now. I told them everything, right down to the names I heard, the addresses I thought I'd been taken to, everything."

Graham could barely believe what he was hearing. "But

they never contacted the British authorities," he said. "There wasn't a *word* about you."

"Good! I made them promise not to."

"But *why*?" Graham asked. It came out as a desperate plea. "Why would you want to stay here and not go home to your family and friends? Or even let them know you're alive?"

She made him wait for an answer, looking out of the window again. "They've got this special unit, for informants or witnesses, whatever you'd call me, and they cut me a deal."

"A *deal*?" Graham asked. The very thought that Beth had been free but unwilling to let her family and friends know, bothered him intensely. *Not every daughter gets the chance to come back and make her parents' lives whole again.*

"I asked for a passport, a new identity, the lease on this place," she said, glancing at the kitchen, "and some money."

"And in return?" Graham asked.

"I helped them take down a bunch of sickos. They're all in jail now," she said, simply.

"A trafficking ring." Graham said gravely. "You took a huge risk, testifying against them."

"I guess. But it was a good deal, and I knew I had to take it. There's no way I could go home, not after all this."

"But why not? Gorey is full of people who love and miss you."

She shook her head. "They *did*. But what would they say to me now? What looks would I get in the street? What would they mutter to each other down at the pub?"

Graham said nothing. He wanted to think the best of the community, but he had to concede that Beth would have had the most difficult time. The story of her abduction would follow her everywhere, through college, and into job interviews and the workplace.

"It would have taken time, but they'd have got over it," he said. But in his heart, he knew how ambitious that was.

"No, no they wouldn't. They are small town people. I would have had years of strange encounters with old friends, people who could barely look me in the eye. There would be rumors. Terrible, awful, lurid rumors. And then I'd have left anyway and started somewhere new. At least I know that I like it here. The people are kind. It's cold and dark in the winter, but I'm used to that, now."

After a long moment's thought, Graham admitted, "Perhaps you're right. There's bravery and standing up for the truth, and then there's having to live your life, knowing every day what people are secretly thinking about you. I wouldn't wish such a life on anyone."

He closed his notebook. "But what about your mother?"

Another shake of the head. Graham saw that this was an issue long since decided in Beth's mind. For him, her mother was real and present, someone they'd spoken to and investigated. But for this brave young woman, Ann was the distant past, to be set aside and forgotten. "You know, I did look her up. I saw that she'd moved and had a larger house. Probably three times what our old family home was worth. Her and Chris could never have afforded one like that. So, I had a look on that 'street view' thing on the Internet. And I saw those posters in the window. About the foundation."

Graham nodded. "They're still there, in her window."

"That's not a foundation or a charity," Beth said, her voice bitter now, "or anything to do with finding me. That's an *advertisement* for attention on behalf of a lonely, scared old woman who never learned how to make her own way."

Graham was silent, letting Beth's pent-up anger flow.

"My mother was always so insecure, always presenting this image of herself as the perfect parent, hostess, and backbone of the local community. But cross her, and she'd turn into witch. Most people wouldn't believe the things she said to me when I didn't do or say or look as she wanted. If I didn't support this image of her that she so badly needed to uphold, I was nothing to her. She needed a husband for that image, too, but the first got himself sent down, and the second was a no-hoper. And then he died, didn't he?"

"Yes, two years ago," Graham told her.

Beth showed no grief whatsoever at this piece of news. "All the more reason for her to lean on people, to guilt them into helping her. Did you know the foundation's website reckons they've got 'active investigations' going on?"

"Yes, we saw that," Graham said.

"Well, here I am!" she exclaimed. "You found me after a bit of good police work. *Ten years later*, my mum's 'investigators' haven't been within a hundred miles of me. There's been no one asking questions or trying to get me to come home or anything. You should arrest her."

"You *want* us to arrest your own mother?"

"She's spent ten years dining out on the worst thing that ever happened to me. I'd say she deserves what's coming to her."

Graham conceded the point. "Beth, we're ready to take action against your mother, but what do you want us to tell her about you?"

She shrugged. "As little as possible." She had calmed down now. She fidgeted for a moment. "Tell her I'm alive. That I'm happy. And that I'm never coming home."

Graham's first instinct was to try to help put the family back together, to act as a mediator between an angry daughter and a deeply flawed mother, but he knew utter conviction when he saw it, and he let the thought pass without comment.

"I have someone else with me. He is waiting outside."

"Who is he?" Beth asked. "Another cop?"

Graham nodded. "We both spent time with your mother, investigating what might have happened to you, and... The other officer is a friend of yours. The young man I believe you used to call 'Bug.'"

Beth was stunned far beyond words.

"Would you like me to call him? I know he'd love to see you again."

She managed, at length, to nod slightly. Graham saw a flicker of guileless innocence cross her face. He pressed a button to send the text he'd prepared earlier.

"Beth... or Bettina, if you'd prefer?"

"Beth..." she cleared her throat, "Call me Beth."

The intercom buzzed. Beth rose to walk across the room and press the button on a wall panel by the door. She looked at the small grey box, hesitating for a moment before glancing up at the ceiling, her hand in mid-air as though considering the wisdom of what she was about to do. Then she covered the button with her finger, giving it a long, definitive press. She said nothing as she returned to her stool.

"It's been ten years," she said, "and I look a sight."

"Please don't worry. He'll just be so glad to see that you're alright."

She was at the door before the knock came, and then it was open, and she was beaming shyly at him. "Hey, Bug."

Roach's eyes shone. "Hey, Barbie."

Graham averted his eyes during the very long hug that followed. His eyes lighted on the joint languishing forgotten in the ashtray. His hand gave a tiny twitch.

"I can't believe it." Roach pulled back to look at her. "You're even prettier than you used to be."

"Oh, stop it," Beth said, waving him away. "You're *tall*," she marveled. "I'd never have thought it."

"Give a man ten years, and he'll grow a bit," Roach said, before dropping his voice, his expression serious. "We've all been so worried about you. Out of our minds."

Beth made to speak, but Roach shushed her, looking at her carefully. "You don't have to say anything now, if you don't want to."

She waved him over to the much-abused leather couch, and there they sat, catching up on old times and old friends. Tactfully, Graham made his way outside for a breath of fresh air, although if he were honest, he'd much have preferred a cup of tea.

An hour later, Graham knocked on the apartment door.

"We have to make a move. We have a plane to catch."

"Yes, of course," Beth replied, and Roach made a move for the door. "You say you've got Lyon under arrest?"

"Yes," Graham said. "We think we can get him between six and eight years in jail for his Internet crimes, especially if we get the right jury and a judge who takes a sufficiently dim view of that sort of thing. We could get more, if you would..."

Beth ignored him but reached for Roach and pulled him into a hug. "Thanks for coming. It was so good to see you."

"You too." Jim whispered. He blinked rapidly, his lips trembling. "Take care, Barbie."

"One last thing, Inspector," Beth turned to Graham.

"You're wrong about one thing. It wasn't Mr. Lyon who kidnapped me."

Graham stared at her, time standing still.

"Then who did?"

"Mr. Grant. He's the headmaster now, I believe."

CHAPTER TWENTY-NINE

ONCE AGAIN, GRAHAM, Roach, and Harding worked through the night. They called in Jack, and he sat alongside them in a t-shirt and sweatpants, having been brought from his bed.

Before they left Copenhagen, Beth had told Graham what happened.

"He did his student teacher training at our school the previous year. He had digs with Mrs. Devizes, two streets down from ours and would sometimes walk home with me if I'd stayed late to do my homework in the library. When he joined the school as a teacher the following year, I didn't have classes with him, but that morning, I recognized his voice. It was definitely him. Irish."

After a consultation with the Chief Constable, a pre-dawn raid was swiftly executed at the home of the headmaster of Gorey Grammar.

Graham and Harding led the charge, backed up by three constables drafted in at short notice from St. Helier. They found Grant asleep in bed. He put up no resistance and was driven away quietly from his home without disturbing the neighbors.

Now, Graham looked at him from across the table in the interview room. Next to Graham sat Janice Harding. The headmaster looked bleary-eyed and was blinking rapidly, the early morning light catching the gray in his stubble. His hands, placed one on top of the other, were on the table, relaxed.

"So, Mr. Grant, tell me about your association with Beth Ridley."

"There is none. I told you before, I never taught her."

"But you lived near to her, did you not?"

"Gorey is a small place. Everyone lives close to one another here."

"You are obfuscating. Why would you do that, Mr. Grant?"

"Oh, I'm sorry. I don't mean to. Must be the early hour. I'm happy to help however I can, but I fear that isn't much."

"So you keep saying. You have nothing to do with Beth Ridley's disappearance, then?"

"Of course not. Absolutely none."

Graham turned over a page that was in a folder in front of him. He wanted to keep this interview moving. Grant had had a long time to perfect his story.

"Tell me about your movements on the morning of her disappearance."

The headmaster let out a deep breath. He started to explain. "It was just an ordinary day. I got up. I was renting a room on Bryony Road. Had my usual breakfast of cereal and a mug of tea, then I left for work. I was an English teacher back then. It was my first year."

"What time did you leave the house?"

"I always got up at seven and liked to be at school by

eight to prepare my classroom before school started. It was about a twenty minute walk so I'd always leave at seven forty, or thereabouts."

Graham got out his phone and looked on a map, tracing the route from Bryony Road to the school.

"The majority of your route was the same as Beth's, including the spot at which she disappeared."

"So? I repeat, I had nothing to do with her disappearance. I didn't even see her."

"You didn't see her." Graham repeated. "Did you see the leg?"

"The leg?"

"Yes, the leg of the doll that was left in the street. The only trace of Beth that was left behind."

"No," Grant replied. "I had already been and gone from that spot by the time she went missing."

"So you didn't see Beth at all?"

"No."

"Okay, tell me about your phone records."

With Jack's help, they had gathered Grant's phone records from ten years ago. It had been a feat of almost superhuman endurance taking nearly the whole night, but he'd eventually cracked it, to Janice's delight and Graham's eternal gratitude.

"They show you made a phone call at 8:16 on that morning. What was that about?"

"I forget. It was a long time ago. Nothing important."

"But a student from your school disappearing isn't a common occurrence. Surely you remember what happened that morning."

"No, sorry. Not that."

Graham rapidly switched tack again.

"Your bank records, Mr. Grant."

"Yes, what about them?"

"You were badly in debt, weren't you? Why was that?"

"Oh, you know, I was young. Living beyond my means, student debt, that kind of thing. That's all an unpleasant memory, now."

Graham looked hard at the man across the table. Grant was wearing a pair of jeans and a red t-shirt that advertised a local hardware store across his chest. On his feet were flip-flops. His hair was short, and he looked a little disheveled after his rude awakening, but otherwise he seemed unruffled. He didn't show any signs of anxiety or concern. Certainly nothing that Graham would like to see. Some sign of guilt.

"Brand new teacher to headmaster in ten years, Mr. Grant. That's some ambition you've got there."

"Not really. Not if you work hard and get some lucky breaks. I've been very fortunate."

"What drives you, Mr. Grant? What are your ambitions?"

"Oh, you know, same as most other people, I expect. A nice house, car, professional respect. I like to see the kids get a good education."

Grant said this all with a straight face, looking directly at Graham.

"Okay, Mr. Grant. We'll leave it there for a while. Let's take a break. I'll come back for a chat later."

Graham switched the tape off and left the room. As he walked into his office, he fought the impulse to punch the filing cabinet.

"He's not giving us an inch, sir. What's the next step?" Harding said.

"Give me a timeline, Sergeant."

"Well sir, we know that Beth left the house just after

eight o'clock. Updike saw her at 8:15. Susan normally met her at 8:20 but she didn't show up. Everything points to her going missing in the intervening five minute period between being seen by Updike and not arriving at her meeting point. The location of the doll's leg confirms it, sir."

"What about Grant?"

"Sir?"

"His timeline. What do we know about that?"

"He left the house at 7:40. Got into school at eight."

"He made the phone call at—?"

"Sixteen minutes past eight, sir."

Graham stood at the window of his office and tapped the wooden frame furiously with his pen. Harding wisely waited.

Then, without a word, Graham took off. Harding watched as he grabbed his jacket and walked out into the reception area.

"Roach?" he barked.

"Yes, sir!" Roach stood to attention at the sound of the DI's voice as he strode across the room.

"Keys!"

Roach spun around, taking the keys to the police vehicle from their hook and throwing them smartly across the room. He watched with satisfaction as his boss caught them equally smartly with one hand and strode out of the station without stopping.

CHAPTER THIRTY

G RAHAM DROVE SWIFTLY, and as he passed through the gates of Gorey Grammar, he looked around for the visitor parking spaces. He jumped out of the car and quickly trotted up the steps to the school.

Inside, he made his way to the school secretary's office and rapped on the door. Mrs. Gates looked up from her computer screen.

"DI Graham! Good to see you again. Can I help you with anything?"

"I certainly hope so, Mrs. Gates.

"You didn't see Mr. Grant outside, did you? School has started, and there's no sign of him. No message either. Most unlike him. I'm getting worried."

Graham sidestepped her question, not wanting to impart that he knew exactly where her employer was.

"Mrs. Gates, what time does Mr. Grant typically make it in?"

"Oh, he's normally here at eight. We get in around the same time. We're both creatures of habit.

"Who opens up the school?"

"The caretaker unlocks the school and classrooms, but Mr. Grant and I have keys to our own offices. Whichever of us gets in first opens them both. I've worked with my heads of school like that for years."

"I wonder if I can ask you to cast your mind back, Mrs. Gates. To the day Beth Ridley disappeared. What happened that morning?"

"Well, let's see. Most of the teachers pass by my office and say good morning." Mrs. Gates tapped her chin with her forefinger. "It was a long time ago, but of course, I've gone over the day in my mind many times."

Graham let her think in silence, even though he was desperate to hurry her up.

"Mr. Bellevue was off sick. With hindsight, it was an early sign of his heart problem, but we didn't know that then. Oh, it was so embarrassing. You see, I'd forgotten my key! Most unusual! I couldn't open our offices. I had to go home for it. When I got back to school, there were parents and students waiting for me in the corridor outside my office."

"So you missed seeing the teachers come in to work?"

"Yes, most of them."

Graham sighed. He felt the energy drain out of him.

"Except for Mr. Grant."

"Oh?"

"I remember because he walked up the steps with me."

Graham pounced. "And what time was that?"

"8:32 precisely."

"Are you quite sure?" Graham felt blood rush to his face.

"I'm positive. I pride myself on my punctuality and when I saw those parents waiting for me, I looked up at the clock to see how late I was. I had to apologize to them profusely. I've only been late three times in twenty years, so I remember exactly how late I was. Thirty-two minutes."

DI Graham stormed back into the police station.

"Harding! We're going back in."

"Yes, sir!"

Back in the room, Grant jumped as the door to the interview room opened.

"Mr. Grant, you told me earlier that you arrived at school at eight o'clock as usual. Fifteen minutes before the final sighting of Beth Ridley."

"Yes, that's right."

"But you didn't, did you?"

"Didn't what?"

"We have a witness who says you were late that day. She says you didn't arrive until after half past eight. She's prepared to testify to that. What do you say?"

Grant didn't say a thing.

"Mr. Grant, it is in your best interests to tell us exactly what happened that morning."

Still nothing. Grant merely blinked back at him.

Graham tried again, "Mr. Grant, I believe that you were deeply in debt and were looking for a way out. We can place you at the spot where Beth disappeared. You have no alibi. You did, however, make a phone call just after the last sighting of Beth. Were you paid to abduct a girl, Mr. Grant?

"Of course not. What is this?" Grant appealed first to Janice, then to Graham. Beads of sweat began to appear on his upper lip.

Graham looked squarely into Grant's brown eyes. "We

also have Beth's own account of her abduction. She recognized your voice, Mr. Grant. Your accent."

At this, Grant twitched violently.

"She's alive?"

Grant stared at the two police officers in front of him, his eyes switching between them for several moments. His head sunk into his hands. When he looked up again, his face was red, his expression desperate.

Janice and Graham stared back at him, still playing their parts in this game of poker face. Grant turned his face to the wall and closed his eyes before turning back and opening them again. He looked directly at Graham. He still said nothing. Later Graham estimated they faced off for a full thirty seconds.

He began quietly.

"I was using. I started in college. But now I couldn't pay. They needed a girl. A blond girl. They said if I could get one for them, they'd wipe out what I owed. And if I didn't... Well, they didn't specify exactly but you know..." He trailed off. "I thought of Beth. I knew her routine. So I set it up."

"What was the plan?" Graham asked his question quietly.

"They would have a car waiting and I was to call them to initiate the pickup."

"Who were these people?" This time, it was Janice who spoke.

"I don't know, exactly. Contacts of my drug dealer. Cocaine," he added, answering their unspoken question. "On that morning, I left my digs as usual and waited for her. I followed her and made the call when the coast was clear. A car pulled up and I pushed her inside," Grant shrugged.

Janice and Graham waited.

"There was no struggle, but the doll got caught in the

car door. The leg must have come off. I didn't notice. They drove away. That was it."

"What did you do then?"

"I carried on walking to school."

Grant glanced across at Harding, who was looking at him impassively, apparently unmoved by his admission. This seemed to light a fire under Grant. He slammed the table with his palms.

"I was in a bad place, okay? I owed them money. A lot of money. God knows what they would have done to me!" Grant was shouting now. "I didn't have a choice!"

He stopped and lay his head on the table in front of him. The room was silent except for the faint sound of seagulls screeching overhead.

Graham considered for a moment the contrast between the freewheeling, seaside bird and the shaking, terrified wretch before him, but unable to feel any sympathy, he clicked off the tape and left the room.

CHAPTER THIRTY-ONE

AN ELDERLY COUPLE waited patiently in the reception area, trying to ignore the inconsolable wailing coming from the interview room a few yards away.

"I'm sorry to keep you waiting," Constable Roach told them, doing his best to bring some brightness to the room amid the sound of the woman's distress. "I'm hoping for a call back from the pound in a moment, and they'll confirm with you that the dog is yours."

"He's never run off before," the old man said. "Always been a good dog."

"We'll have him back to you in a couple of hours," Roach assured him. The phone was ringing yet again. It had been, by any standards, an extremely busy morning.

The wailing showed no signs of stopping. "Oh, for Pete's sake," Roach muttered under his breath. "Calm down, will you?"

Ann Leach was going through the unimaginable. Just after breakfast, she'd found herself arrested for fraud. An hour later, she'd been shown a picture of her daughter, smiling and confident with sparkling blue eyes and multi-colored hair. From the fragments of speech that Sergeant Harding had managed to understand, what had most upset Mrs. Leach was this second cruel loss of her daughter; that she was alive but refused to see her mother.

Harding left the interview room, unable to bear another moment. It had been a lengthy and genuine outpouring of emotion from Ann Leach.

Initially, Janice had managed some sympathy for her, but after an hour's solid wailing, even her patience was wearing thin.

"I don't mean to be unkind," Roach began.

"But she needs to get a grip?" Janice said. "You're telling me. Who've we got in reception?"

"Couple whose dog wandered off and was growling at school kids at the bus stop. The animal unit from Bouley Bay picked it up. They'll be reunited shortly."

Janice gave him a smile. "Pretty mundane after all this, isn't it?" she said, nodding toward the interview room.

DI Graham emerged from his office and stretched. He looked tired. After picking up Grant, they'd moved on Ann, and by ten o'clock that morning, she was in custody.

Ann had found herself, all in the same hour, charged with fraud, informed that her daughter was alive, and told that Beth would not be visiting. Not today. Not ever.

Graham paused at the desk. "Everything alright?"

Another wail of grief and sadness erupted from the interview room.

Graham winced. "Yeah," he said simply, answering his own question. "What's the name of the psychologist chap we called in after that death at the castle?"

"I'll call him," Janice said.

"Any more news about Lyon?" Roach asked his boss.

"Well, his transfer to the mainland went off without a hitch, and the CPS thinks we've got a winner. They reckon they can put together enough to get him eight years, maybe ten, for the Internet stuff."

While Roach and Graham had been in Denmark, Jack Wentworth had completed a forensic examination of Lyon's hard drive. On it, he'd recovered deleted files that proved conclusively that Lyon had received, downloaded, and viewed illegal images.

"Serves him bloody well right," Roach said.

"I have to tell you though, his face was a picture when I told him he was no longer a murder suspect," Graham said. "Sutton looked so relieved that you'd have thought he'd been facing jail time himself."

"Maybe he should," Janice opined, the phone to her ear as she waited for the psychologist's office to pick up.

"He was just doing his job," Graham reminded her.

Roach noticed a vehicle pulling up outside. "Third transfer van of the day. You don't see that very often around here."

Together, the three of them ushered Ann Leach to the waiting vehicle. They eschewed handcuffs. She was visibly too weak and distressed to do anything other than what she was told. As Graham made to close the doors, she said, "I'm sorry. Really. I know I've done wrong. But you've got to let me see my daughter!"

Graham closed the first of the two doors. "Not our decision to make, Mrs. Leach." He closed the second door and knocked on the van's chassis to let the driver know he could head out.

Graham went inside and spent half an hour simply sitting at his desk. With the dog emergency resolved, he, Roach and Harding found themselves with little to do.

"Have we heard from Grace Darling this morning?" Graham asked. Janice caught the reference, but Roach had to quickly Google it.

"He's taken the day off," Janice reported. "Said he'd never been so cold in all his life. The lifeboat captain said he nearly drowned, sir."

Roach scratched his chin. "I can't believe I'm suggesting this, sir, but do you think it'd be entirely out of line for... well, you know..."

"An official commendation?" Graham finished arching an eyebrow. "Seems appropriate to me. What do you think, Janice?"

She gave Roach's shoulder a squeeze. "A couple of those are in order, if you ask me," she smiled. "Just don't let it go to your head, Roachie."

"And in the meantime, dinner?" Graham asked. "Seven o'clock? Bangkok Palace?"

"As long as you're buying," Janice said.

"I'm in," Roach added.

"Great. Now, go and find some police work to do. I've got to make a phone call."

Graham thought for a long moment before dialing the number. In every investigation, there were red herrings and missteps, but he felt the need to apologize.

"Mrs. Updike? I'm so sorry to bother you again. This is DI Graham from Gorey Constabulary, down in Jersey... Yes, that's right... No, please don't worry. Is your husband there? I'd like you both to hear this, you see... No, there's no trouble at all, I assure you. Quite the opposite, actually. I have some very good news for you both."

The waiter gave Graham a worried look. "Sir, please. The chef uses Thai chilies. Extremely hot." The waiter was new.

Graham folded up the menu and handed it back. "Yes, I understand."

"He adds a small *pile* of them to the pan, sir. Not just one or two."

"And I'm saying that I'd like it just the way he'd make it for himself," Graham specified once more.

The waiter dithered but couldn't leave the table without dispensing another warning. "Sir... Management can't be held responsible for any—"

"Don't worry, son, honestly. I won't sue if I explode."

The waiter made a note on his pad. He trotted back to the kitchen, muttering to himself in his native language.

Janice stared at him. "This isn't some weird, macho competition, is it?"

"Huh?"

"I mean, Constable Barnwell nearly loses his life saving a drowning teenager, so you feel the need to prove your manhood by eating fatal levels of Thai spice."

"Don't be ridiculous," Graham said. "I just like a bit of zing in my Asian food, that's all."

Marcus Tomlinson shared their concern, but he'd at least watched Graham handle what the chef called the "five-chili special" variant of his chicken with holy basil, and that unforgettable red curry, which a stunned reviewer from the *Gorey Herald* later memorably described as "part traditional curry, part nuclear treaty violation."

Graham raised his glass. "I have some people to thank," he said. "First, Constable Barnwell, the hero of the hour..."

The whole table – Harding, Roach, Tomlinson, Jack Wentworth, and the RNLI lifeboat captain, Will Ryan – warmly applauded the slightly red-faced constable.

"... for his devotion to duty, selflessness in the face of danger, and successful rescue of a very reckless, very..."

"Stupid," Ryan chipped in, good-naturedly.

"... lucky," Graham continued, "young man. I'd also like to thank the perceptive and persistent Constable Roach..."

More applause and table-thumping were his reward.

"... for his remarkably keen eye, especially when it comes to young women long since thought lost to us." Everyone got a kick out of that, but for Roach, it was bittersweet.

"And, not to be outdone, the potent new team of Harding and Wentworth for their sterling work in tracking down a dangerous predator and then uncovering a decade of fraud. I thank you all, most sincerely. It's a privilege to work with such able and dedicated professionals."

Dishes arrived with steaming platters of fried rice. Graham found himself in a debate with Wentworth about the "Snooper's Charter," while Barnwell was forced yet again to recount the story of his remarkable journey on the *George Sullivan*, complete with Captain Ryan's derogatory remarks about the erstwhile crew of the *Sea Witch*.

"What in the seven hells were they doing in that old wreck of a boat, anyway?" Ryan wanted to know. "They'd have both died in that cold water if we'd taken much longer to get there."

Barnwell had heard the boys' story from Charlie as they'd sat under warm blankets in the ambulance that had picked them up upon their return to dry land. "They were skipping their exams," he explained, "and planned to sail to the French coast. There they'd ditch the boat and hitchhike their way to the South of France and on to Spain. They thought they'd get work in bars down in one of the resorts."

Ryan guffawed at this. "Silly buggers. They'd have been

recruited as drug mules as soon as they got short of money. Are they going to pay for all those thefts, then?"

Barnwell swallowed his massaman curry before answering. "I'm thinking of recommending to the magistrate that they be given community service down at the marina," he reported. "Helping paint the older boats, clean up after the seagulls, that kind of thing." Ryan seemed content with this.

"You know," Roach said, "it's impossible to ignore how important computers were in this whole business. But I think I really learned something about police work, too."

"Oh?" Graham asked. The red curry had brought him to the point of sweating but not yet to the acute discomfort he secretly feared.

"Well, I wouldn't have spotted Beth if I hadn't been prepared to put the time in," he noted. "No software could have found her. Just someone who was looking for the right things."

Janice nodded. "And while we *used* the Internet a lot, we had to know what we were looking for. That required a human brain."

"So," Graham summed up, dabbing his mouth with his napkin, "I need not worry, quite yet, that police officers are about to be replaced with heartless robots?"

"Not *quite* yet," Harding agreed. "A good pair of eyes and a thoughtful mind can do an awful lot, still."

"Doesn't hurt to have a decent mentor, either," Roach observed.

Graham just smiled. The arrests were his reward, along with the knowledge that they'd done the right thing in a case that had been too long ignored. He felt pride, too. In his officers and in his methods. And there was no harm, he decided, in letting that show just a little.

Later after they'd all finished their food, chattered, and

laughed themselves hoarse, the events of the last forty-eight hours began to take their toll.

"Right, then," Graham said, finishing his drink and rising. "I'm going to head off before things get out of hand here. Marcus? Can I give you a lift?" He signaled for the check. When it arrived, the waiter inquired three separate times about Graham's health. "Really, I'm fine. I think the chef went easy on me."

"Please, sir. Call us tomorrow, and let us know you're okay."

Barnwell left next, offering Captain Ryan a ride to his coastal cottage, and Roach headed for his bicycle, chained to the railing outside the restaurant. Janice and Jack were left alone at the table.

"Last pair standing," Jack observed. "Would you like anything else? Maybe we could share some dessert?"

Janice felt herself blush a little and glanced away for a moment. Then she smiled at Wentworth, and realized just how much she was beginning to enjoy his honesty and that friendly, expressive face of his. "Sure," she said finally, her eyes meeting his. "That sounds nice."

EPILOGUE

AFTER HER DEFENSE successfully cited Ann Leach's emotional distress as a factor in her crimes, she was convicted of fraud but received a suspended prison sentence. Leach was also ordered never to attempt to travel to Denmark, where she was blacklisted by the immigration authorities. She had no contact with her daughter. After her trial Ann moved away from Gorey and to Wiltshire, where she took work in a small hotel.

The members of the Gorey community were shocked, saddened, and in some cases angered by the revelations resulting from the police investigation into the Beth Ridley Foundation. A committee was set up by a local council member to discover whether any of the funds could be recovered, but after ten months of rancor and no progress, the matter was quietly dropped.

Andrew Lyon was sentenced to seven years and three months for possessing, distributing, and financially benefiting from the distribution of indecent images of minors. His time in prison has been marked by a campaign of intimidation and violence toward him by other inmates. His repeated requests to be moved to a different prison have been ignored. He is on constant suicide watch. On his release, he will be placed on the Violent and Sex Offenders Register (ViSOR) and never allowed to work with children again.

Despite a confession, the Crown Prosecution Service felt the evidence to support a conviction in the case against Liam Grant for the kidnapping and trafficking of Beth Ridley was not conclusive. The case was never brought to trial. Grant resigned from his post at Gorey Grammar and moved back to his native Ireland. He died in a car crash six months later.

Mr. and Mrs. Updike received a Royal Mail Special Delivery three weeks after Andrew Lyon's arrest. It was a rare and much sought-after invitation card from 1868, sent to a noted politician of the day, requesting the pleasure of his company for a late supper with Queen Victoria. The invitation immediately took pride of place in the Updikes' collection. The card accompanying the gift said simply, "Best regards, DG."

Constable Barnwell was presented with the Queen's Gallantry Medal for his sea rescue of Charlie Hodgson. He remains friends with the teen's parents, for whom he has become something of a mentor. Since his experience on the *George Sullivan*, Barnwell has signed up for lifesaving lessons.

Charlie Hodgson and Rob Boyle were arrested upon their return to Gorey in the *George Sullivan*. The jury heard an honest recounting of the boys' plans to skip three "terrifying" school exams scheduled for the following week and instead sail to the French coast and from there head to Spain. They were found guilty of eight offenses and sentenced to sixty hours of Community Service at the Gorey Marina. Having impressed Captain Smith with his attention to detail and punctuality, Rob was offered an apprenticeship on Smith's fishing trawler and spent three weeks in the mid-Atlantic. Charlie returned to school and was later accepted onto a vocational college course to learn boat restoration.

For his work on the Ridley case, Mrs. Taylor decided to give DI Graham a generous discount on the next month's rent of his room at the White House Inn. She also continued, with a quiet determination, to have his path somehow cross with that of an eligible young woman.

Jim Roach received a police commendation for diligence and persistence in the Beth Ridley case. His framed certificate sits on the mantelpiece above the fireplace in his mother's home. He now regularly starts for the Jersey Police five-a-side squad. There are high hopes that the team will win the league this year.

Bettina Nisted got married in the summer. She and her husband Johann are expecting their first child early next year.

Janice and Jack shared a leisurely dessert and sat talking for well over an hour after the last diners had departed the *Bangkok Palace*. They were seen strolling slowly down the road, hand in hand, talking together as though neither wanted the evening to end. As he locked up and cleared their table, the headwaiter was delighted to find a generous tip. As he pocketed it, he reflected on the fact that unlike their older dining companion, he would not need to consider the young couple's wellbeing when he woke the following morning.

To get your free copy of *The Case of the Screaming Beauty,* the prequel to the Inspector David Graham series, plus two more books, updates about new releases, exclusive promotions, and other insider information, sign up for Alison's mailing list at:

https://www.alisongolden.com/graham

INSPECTOR DAVID GRAHAM WILL RETURN...

WHAT HAPPENS NEXT for our intrepid team in the Bailiwick of Jersey? Find out in the next book in the Inspector Graham cozy mystery series, *The Case of the Missing Letter*. You'll find an excerpt on the following pages.

THE CASE OF THE MISSING LETTER

CHAPTER ONE

DAVID GRAHAM TROTTED downstairs. The dining room was becoming busier by the week, but at least his favorite table by the window was still available on this bright Saturday morning. The White House Inn staff were busier than they had been since Christmas, welcoming and looking after new arrivals who had chosen to exchange the snow of Scotland or the dreary rain of Manchester for a few sunny days in Jersey. He took his seat and opened the morning paper, part of a reassuring and established routine he had enjoyably been following for the last six months.

As he settled into life on Jersey, Graham had followed the changing of the seasons as the island's surprisingly mild winter gave way to an even warmer and quite invigorating early spring. By mid-March, the island was once again beginning to look its splendid and colorful best. The spring blooms were out. Swathes of bright yellow daffodils and the unmistakable, bell-shaped blue hyacinth dotted the island. Economically, Jersey had also started to blossom. Most of Gorey's small fishing fleet had completed a month of refit and repair. Shortly, they would be heading out among the

Channel Islands to catch lobster and oysters, or further into the Atlantic for cod.

"Good morning, Detective Inspector," Polly offered carefully. Before his first cup of tea, Graham could be sleepy and even uncharacteristically sour. Guesthouse owner, the redoubtable Mrs. Taylor, occasionally reminded staff not to engage him in anything beyond perfunctory morning pleasantries before he was at least partially caffeinated. "What will it be today? Or are you going to make me guess again?"

Graham peered over his newspaper at the freckled twenty-something redhead who had become perhaps his favorite of the staff. "I have to say, Polly," Graham told her, folding the paper and setting it on the table, "that you're becoming something of a psychic. What is it now, four correct guesses in a row?"

"Five," Polly said proudly. "But on three of those days, it was that new Assam you were so excited about."

"True, true," Graham noted. "And I hope you'll agree it was worth getting excited over."

Polly shrugged. "I'm not really a tea drinker," she confessed. "But today I'm going to guess you're in... what do you call it sometimes... a 'traditional mood'?"

"I might be," Graham grinned. "Or I might be feeling spontaneous."

"Lady Grey," Polly guessed. "Large pot, two bags, sugar to be decided on a cup-by-cup basis."

Impressed, Graham raised his eyebrows and gave her a warm smile. "Precisely. I don't know how you do it."

Polly tapped her forehead cryptically and sashayed off to the kitchen to place Graham's order. Since arriving at the White House Inn, and with the enthusiastic support of the staff and Mrs. Taylor, Graham had taken sole "curatorial control" over the dining room's tea selection. He took this role exceptionally seriously. The kitchen's shelves were now stocked with an impressive array of Asian teas, from the sweet and fruity to the fragranced and flowery, with much else in between.

Lady Grey, though, was becoming Graham's favorite "first pot." It was often given the responsibility of awakening the Detective Inspector's mental faculties first thing in the morning. It was in the moments after the first life-giving infusion of caffeine, antioxidants, and other herbal empowerments that Graham's mind came alive.

One useful byproduct of his daily tea ritual was the ability to memorize almost everything he read. His knowledge of local events was becoming peerless. With the aid of the local newspaper, Graham stored away the information that Easter was two weekends away, and the town's churches were inviting volunteers to bake, sing, decorate the church, and organize the Easter egg hunts.

Also stashed away for future retrieval was the nugget that Gorey Castle's much anticipated "Treason and Torture" exhibit was about to open. The gruesome displays were only part of the attraction, however. Two recently opened chambers had, until their inadvertent discovery a few months earlier, contained an unlikely and entirely unsuspected trove of artistic treasures. The discovered paintings had mostly been returned to their owners or loaned to museums that were better equipped to display pieces of such importance. But, interest in the find was still high, and ticket sales had been, to quote the Castle's events director, the ever-upbeat Stephen Jeffries, "brisk beyond belief."

"Lady Grey," Polly announced, delivering the tray with

Graham's customary digital timer which was just passing the three-minute mark.

"First class, Polly. And it'll be bacon, two eggs, and toast today, please."

"Right, you are," she nodded.

Graham put the paper aside and focused on this most pleasing of ceremonies. First came the tea, promisingly dark and full-bodied, tumbling into the china cup. Then came the enchanting aroma, an endless complexity from such a surprisingly simple source. Next would come the careful decision-making process regarding the addition of milk; too much would bring down the temperature, and as Graham liked to think of it, risked muddling what the tea was attempting to express.

Finally, he would add just the right amount of sugar. Graham had taken pains to instruct the wait staff to ensure that it was available in loose, as well as cubed form, so that he might more carefully adjudicate its addition. He tipped an eighth of a teaspoonful into the cup and stirred nine times, counter-clockwise. Some things, as he was so fond of reminding his fellow police officers, are worth doing well. He chose to ignore their barely suppressed eye-rolls.

He took a sip and cherished the added bergamot that complemented the traditional Earl Grey flavor. But then, contrary to his usual practice, Graham set down the cup. An article on page six of the newspaper was demanding his attention. The headline was *Our Cops are Tops*, and he read on with a quiet flush of pride.

After their successes in recent months, it goes without saying that Gorey has the most capable police officers on the island. Led by the indefatigable Detective Inspector Graham, the Gorey Constabulary has successfully raised the rate at which it solves reported crimes from twenty-six percent, one year ago, to forty-nine percent, today.

"For once," Graham muttered contentedly into his paper, "the media have got their numbers spot-on." It meant, he had observed proudly to his team the previous day, that anyone planning a crime in their small field of jurisdiction would know that they had a one in two chance of getting caught. "Splendid."

Moreover, the actual crime rate has dropped by sixteen percent in the last twelve months. This is surely cause to congratulate DI Graham and his team, but Sergeant Janice Harding was modest when asked for a comment. "The Gorey public have been enormously supportive," she pointed out. "We rely on their vigilance and common sense, and they've stood by us through some complex and challenging cases." The popular sergeant, who has lived on Jersey for nearly seven years, was referring to the conviction of former teacher Andrew Lyon, who began a seven-year sentence at Wormwood Scrubs in January. Gorey Constabulary also met with success after murder investigations at the Castle and the White House Inn. It seems our "top cops" are equal to any challenge. Gorey is fortunate to have such a dedicated and dependable crime-fighting team.

"'Top cops.' Sounds like one of those ghastly TV reality shows," Graham grumbled. "But I'll take it."

To get your copy of The Case of the Missing Letter, visit the link below:
https://www.alisongolden.com/missing-letter

BOOKS BY ALISON GOLDEN

FEATURING REVEREND ANNABELLE DIXON

Death at the Café (Prequel)

Murder at the Mansion

Body in the Woods

Grave in the Garage

Horror in the Highlands

Killer at the Cult

FEATURING DIANA HUNTER

Hunted (Prequel)

Snatched

Stolen

Chopped

Exposed

ABOUT THE AUTHOR

Alison Golden is the *USA Today* bestselling author of the Inspector David Graham mysteries and Reverend Annabelle Dixon cozy mysteries. As A.J. Golden, she writes the Diana Hunter thriller series.

Alison was raised in Bedfordshire, England. Her aim is to write stories that are designed to entertain, amuse, and calm. Her approach is to combine creative ideas with excellent writing and edit, edit, edit.

Alison is based in the San Francisco Bay Area with her husband and twin sons. She splits her time between London and San Francisco.

For up-to-date promotions and release dates of upcoming books, sign up for the latest news here: https://www.alisongolden.com/graham.

For more information:
www.alisongolden.com
alison@alisongolden.com

facebook.com/alisongolden.books

twitter.com/alisonjgolden

instagram.com/alisonjgolden

THANK YOU

Thank you for taking the time to read *The Case of the Broken Doll*. If you enjoyed it, please consider telling your friends or posting a short review. Word of mouth is an author's best friend and very much appreciated.

Thank you,

CPSIA information can be obtained
at www.ICGtesting.com
Printed in the USA
LVHW110248261219
641710LV00001B/244/P